Current
Climate

Friedman   6.50

The
Current
Climate

Also by Bruce Jay Friedman

The Current Climate

A NOVEL BY
Bruce Jay Friedman

A MORGAN ENTREKIN BOOK
THE ATLANTIC MONTHLY PRESS
NEW YORK

Published simultaneously in Canada
Printed in the United States of America

Library of Congress Cataloging-in-Publication Data
Friedman, Bruce Jay, 1930–
The current climate : a novel / by Bruce Jay Friedman.
"A Morgan Entrekin book."
ISBN 0-87113-276-1
I. Title.

PS3556.R5C87   1989   89-31500   813'.54—dc20

Design by Laura Hough

The Atlantic Monthly Press
19 Union Square West
New York, NY 10003

FIRST PRINTING

For Jack and Bob and David and Leslie and Carl and Jimmy and Elaine—and company.

*. . . later, when he had been "reduced back to a writer,"
he often wondered if his plan was secretly followed. . . .*

F. Scott Fitzgerald
The Pat Hobby Stories

The
Current
Climate

One

∿∿ ABOUT HALFWAY ALONG IN THE MEET-ing, Harry Towns could tell it was not going to work out. The network executives were polite, attentive. They even threw in an encouraging chuckle here and there. The woman with the man's name leaned forward, as if she were right on the edge of excitement. But the executive who was known as the Inquisitor didn't ask any questions. He kept his eyes lowered and scribbled notes. In the corridor, the agent said he felt it had "gone well." Yes, the executives had the power to okay the show then and there, but sometimes they didn't. Sometimes they wanted to kick it around "internally." As it turned out, Harry was right—the executives had just been going through the motions.

He had been pitching a show in which the main character was a dog. He used that as an example of how low he had sunk. "A dog show," he had told a friend. "It's come to that." But he had gotten to like that dog show. He imagined himself doing five years' worth of it and never getting tired of the sucker. As it turned out, the network had a similar show in development. One with a famous dog. That meant he had made the trip for nothing. Two and a half hours to the airport, a couple more sitting on the ground, then five in the air. Not to speak of getting up for the meeting. He hadn't gone to one for a while, so naturally he was rusty. He had to remember to be focused but also a little casual, so as not to give the impression that it was life or death for him.

He had taken six months off to write his famous Spanish Armada play. Famous around his house. The way screenwriters are always going to write a novel someday, he was always going to

3

write a play. He had gotten a few months ahead and finally decided to call his own bluff. The trouble was that the British and the Spanish never really went at each other. They stayed out of each other's range until a storm tore up the Spanish fleet. So it wasn't inherently dramatic. He thought he would jump in and see if he could drum up a little conflict along the way—but he hadn't succeeded. Meanwhile his accountant had called and told him he'd better hurry up and get a payday. If he wanted to keep his house. The accountant had been a little detached. There was a possibility that the fucking accountant might drop him. How would that look?

And now he had to take the trip back—with nothing to show for it. He would call Julie and tell her about it and she'd be cheerful, telling him that something else would come up, it always did. But maybe it wouldn't this time.

It wasn't anyone's fault. These things happened. The networks were secretive about their projects. They probably wanted to see if his notion was different enough from the one they had to justify a go-ahead. It wasn't as if the trip could have been headed off.

He drove back to the hotel feeling bone tired. He had heard people say they felt every one of their years. It was his turn to feel every one of his, plus a few more. They had put him in a hotel of their choice, not his, and he had gone along with it. What was so important about a hotel room? For a quick hit. He told himself it was nice to look out the window and see L.A. from a different angle—but he was aware every second that it was their hotel, not his.

He thought of calling Matty, who would take him to Spago, or Sid, who would take him wherever he wanted to go. They were powerful men. Industry survivors. They had weathered the trends and could always get something going. You could call them at the last second and they wouldn't stand on ceremony. If either was free, he'd say so. Harry could get himself seen that way. He was tired at the moment, but he looked good. He had his own kind of tan, an East Coast tan, and though he had gotten a late start at it, he had become a tennis fanatic. So he had a tennis waist, too, or

4

at least the start of one. There may have been some talk that he was a doper. He had reason to believe that a certain producer had spread that around. Because he had picked up the man and his wife and danced them around a disco. The two of them, off the ground and in his arms. A little error of judgment. Also, there was the new concern about your age. If you were past forty, you were in trouble. You had to come to meetings with a young guy who would act as a beard. And was Harry ever past forty. Cruising along, as he said, in his fifties. What the hell, he was fifty-seven. If he showed up with Matty or Sid, a deal would come up, right on the spot. A studio executive would recognize him and ask him to come by. Or a retired agent would shuffle over with a project—like a punch-drunk fighter answering a bell. And there would be something to it too. He had seen it happen. But not lately.

He had a few notions, too, and had intended to see if any of them would fly—as long as he was in L.A.—but the meeting had stolen his energy. He was pitched out.

He called Julie and told her about the setback and, just as he anticipated, she was cheerful and told him not to worry about it. The thing to do was to go out and have a great time his last night in L.A. Her response was predictable, but what was he complaining about? He had been with some gloombombs and should have known better.

Harry knew a handsome woman in L.A. and had a feeling that he could probably catch her in for dinner. But it had been several years since he had last seen her, and she'd had time to store up some new defeats. He didn't feel he could take them on right now. Then, too, they might get something going, and he would have to fly back feeling awful.

He decided he needed a little home cooking, so to speak, and ended up calling Travis, the one friend he had in L.A. who wasn't in show business. Not that he was entirely innocent. Travis liked the fact that Harry had his name on a couple of big pictures. And he was ready to sign over his house to any woman with even the slightest connection to the entertainment world. Someone who'd been on *Gilligan's Island.* Or even an old girlfriend of Hefner's. That part of his life hadn't gone well.

But everything else had. Travis had come to L.A. some twenty years back—as a pharmacist with shaky credentials—and had proceeded to make a ton of money. Not right off the bat but eventually. And not as a pharmacist but in business deals. Leases, franchises, buy-outs. All of it with a distinctive L.A. stamp to it. Once he had sat with Harry in a darkened car and told him he could make a lot of money for him "offshore." Harry had listened politely, but he had let it go by. That kind of thing had nothing to do with him. Maybe because of the darkened car.

He had a lot of numbers for Travis, but the one he dialed was a central station manned by an assistant whose style was whipped and deferential, even over the phone. He knew who Harry was and how much pleasure Travis got out of the dinners and would see to it that his employer got the message. They set up a date for nine-thirty at the Palm. Harry felt confident that Travis would be there. You could call him at the last minute and usually he'd be available. Not in the way that Matty or Sid would be. With all the money Travis had made, he hadn't been able to get anything substantial going in his personal life. His was a sad kind of availability.

Harry had a minor matter to take care of before dinner. An agent had called and said he wanted him as a client. In the past several years Harry had been represented by a colossal agency, a kind of General Motors, and it hadn't worked out. The arrangement was too vague. He had been warned about the impersonality of such groups, and sure enough, there wasn't a single individual he could really get his hands on. The agent who called said he was just such an individual. So Harry said what the hell, he'd have a drink with him.

The agent certainly looked like a good agent. He had wavy hair and a great mustache. Harry thought he recognized the look from a TV show, one that was slanted demographically toward folks in their thirties, but it still looked good on him. Harry had a double

THE CURRENT CLIMATE

Gibson and began to think it might be nice to have a handsome fellow representing him, one with a nice demographic look about him. And the agent certainly was eager enough. He said he was small but that he would work his ass off. They were joined by a woman colleague. She said she handled the "classy" side of the group's clients, which presumably would include Harry. And she would work her ass off too. So now there were two people willing to work their asses off for him. Harry was starting to figure what the hell, he wasn't going anywhere with the other gang, when the fellow made the remark. He knew about Megan, Towns's four-year-old daughter. He had a five-year-old son.

"If I had you as a client," he said, "my son would always have a little chippy waiting for him back East."

And that was that. Harry said he would think about it when he got back home, but he had already thought about it. No chippy stuff.

Harry was that way. He had canceled out a business manager when the fellow said Towns would be given a "pishy little allowance." Actually Harry had been prepared to allow him one "pishy," but after the second one, it was case closed. He knew what the business manager meant. Walking-around money. But don't call it "pishy."

Travis had him paged at the bar of the Palm and said it was all right about dinner but that he might be a little late. Harry told him not to worry about it, to take his time. They were easy with each other now. Usually Travis tried to fool him on the phone with a Yiddish accent or a Spanish one, but he had dropped that. The accents were getting too easy to pick off.

After waiting at the bar for half an hour, Harry was sorry he had told Travis to take his time. He was ready to eat tables and chairs. Maybe they were being too easy with each other. He looked at the caricatures of celebrities on the wall. When the Palm had first opened, the owner had asked him for his picture and he had never gotten around to sending him one. Now he was sorry he hadn't taken him up on it. At times like this he would be able to look at

7

a caricature of himself on the wall. And the owner had never asked him again.

There were two women at the bar. Harry heard them say they were from Cincinnati. They weren't major leaguers—just two women from Cincinnati. Normally he wouldn't have thought of them that way—not anymore—but this was Hollywood. He shouldered his way into the conversation, telling them he was waiting for a friend who was finishing up a little brain surgery. He had been living in the country for a while, away from the bars, and he was aware that his remarks were strained. But they put up with the intrusion, and by the time Travis arrived, the women were curious about him, even when they found out he wasn't a brain surgeon. Travis fell all over them, giving them every one of his numbers. It was as if he had just gotten out of prison and hadn't seen a woman in years. Harry saw that it was useless to try to pry him away, so he went up ahead to their table and got started with a shrimp cocktail, thinking maybe he had missed his profession.

By the time Travis joined him, the crowd had begun to thin out and they had to rush to get served. Harry ordered veal parmigiana, an unusual call in a steak house, but that's what he was in the mood for. He noticed that Travis dressed differently now. For years he had gone with what Harry thought of as a hairdresser look, the old kind of hairdresser, with his shirt cut low to the waist and heavy chains and white shoes with lifts in them and tassels. He'd worn a lot of orange. And he had come up with an odd color for his hair, one that hadn't quite worked out. But someone had gotten hold of him and told him to lighten up. He wore a soft linen suit and had let his hair get a little gray and comfortable-looking. He seemed less prickly too.

Since they didn't see each other too often, they were able to get a good clean bead on one another. Normally it was Travis who was up against it. Travis, with the sister who freaked out and lived in Cuba. Travis, with the father who surfaced after thirty years and threatened to kill his mother if she didn't take him back. Travis's women. The short, rudderless one with the great body. Should he

8

let her do a split-beaver shot for a skin magazine? It was the first time Towns had ever heard anyone say *split-beaver*. Or Travis's niece, would you believe? She had packed up her children and left her husband for Travis. Was she intelligent enough for him? Or the Polish model who had a roomful of furs but didn't seem to have a visible means of support. Could he trust her? With his credit cards?

Travis couldn't figure out where he went wrong with women. He had once taken a psychiatrist along on a date to see how he interacted with them. An L.A. solution. Harry had introduced Julie to Travis, who immediately perceived her as being a certain kind of parochial-school girl he remembered from his childhood. A type that had nothing to do with her. Nonetheless, he had flown at her with angry theological arguments—the Catholics against the Jews. Later, when Harry suggested that he had acted poorly, Travis had been shocked. He thought he had been charming. So Harry knew about Travis and women.

He would listen to Travis's adventures and try to throw out a helpful comment, at the same time trying not to be smug about it. This was difficult since Travis was rolling around like a loose cannon and Harry was seeing things from the safe compound in which he lived with Julie and Megan. But the work stopped coming and Julie had started to knock them back, and he was so uneasy that he couldn't even enjoy his daughter. So this time around it was Harry's turn to unload.

He told Travis about the trip and how he had come up empty. And how the dice had been running cold for him. About the age thing in Hollywood. And how he couldn't seem to get anything going. He had the credits, and as he was fond of pointing out, they didn't put your name up there because you were Jewish. But it didn't seem to matter. He was perceived as someone who couldn't bring a script over the top. And to an extent it was true. But what was wrong with getting them in sight of the goal line? He had been doing that for years and hadn't had a complaint. But it was different now. They wanted fellows who could take them all the way. He

9

could do that, too, but they weren't giving him a chance. Or who knows, maybe it was the dope rap. Harry didn't use much these days, but he had used a lot back then, used it the night he had picked up the producer and his wife and waltzed them around the disco. The producer had a resigned little pout on his face as he and his wife were whisked off the ground, and who could blame him for being pissed off? He was known as an amoral little prick, but who knows, maybe the fucker had some dignity. Who could blame him for passing it around that Harry was a doper?

When Harry's veal parmigiana came out, it didn't appear to have any veal in it. Or maybe the veal had dissolved in the sauce. It had been that kind of trip. While Harry was deciding whether to send it back or just mop up the parmigiana part with bread, Travis took a quick turn. He was wondering if he should part company with a business associate. He had given the fellow thousands of dollars on ventures that kept going down the drain. He didn't mind that part. "I'm making so much money, anyway," he said. But the fellow kept putting him down. Travis had his eye on a girl, someone who had once done a *Family Ties.* The fellow had told him face it, what would a girl in her twenties see in someone like Travis? Harry picked that one off easily. He told Travis that by definition he shouldn't have anyone in his life who put him down. And then he jumped in quickly and got started on the house, how much it meant to him with the peach trees, and how he would feel if he had to sell it and move Julie and Megan up to Vermont somewhere. He admitted he would be embarrassed about it. He and Travis had known each other since college. The clock was ticking. They could get naked with each other.

"Why didn't you come to me?" Travis asked. "How is anyone supposed to know you're in trouble if you don't ask?"

"I wouldn't be much good at that," said Towns.

But why wouldn't he? For one thing, he didn't know if the offer was meant to be a loan or a gift. He couldn't take a gift, could he? And if it was a loan, what if he didn't pay it back in time? Travis's father had been in the rackets, connected with one of the smaller casinos in Vegas. They had found him eventually under a piano in the lounge, and Travis had to go out to identify the body. So the father was dead. But he probably had associates. You could say that this was Travis, not his father, but Harry remembered his friend in the darkened car whispering about offshore stuff. Also, he had seen some types moving quietly around Travis's house in the hills. Irritable men wearing Arrow shirts and ties in the hot sun. Not official hard noses, but worse in a way.

But that wasn't it. For all he knew, it was a straightforward offer, from the heart and with no strings. What reason did he have to doubt this? It was more a question of Harry not wanting to turn over the wheel. He had to be the one to bring the ball down, pick up the check. He had a few dollars out on the street. He liked to say that: "I have some money on the street." In truth it wasn't much—fifties, hundreds. But he was the one who passed it out. How would it look if he started taking? How would it look if he had to move to Vermont?

At school neither of them had much money, but it was Harry who had bought milk shakes for his skinny friend. Later he was a screenwriter with his name on a couple of big pictures. Travis boasted about having gone to school with him. How would it look if he took money from Travis, who was shorter than he was? Always, it was how would it look.

So he let the offer slide. He had been in trouble before. Something always came up. Fuck the age thing. Could anyone match his original conceptions? When he was on target? Let them enjoy their youth. One of these days he was going to grab one of them and say: "Congratulations on your youth."

He let Travis pick up the check. It was the least he could do. And they went out on the street. Travis was in wonderful condition if you liked that kind of shape. Real tight and drawn. He hit balls every day of his life. He'd gotten up to ten hours a day once until he realized he was having a nervous breakdown. But for the moment, in the streetlight, bent over, with his shoulders bunched up tight, he had the skull of a little old man.

11

Harry was fading, but Travis wanted to keep going. He was almost cranky about it. He didn't get much of a chance to see his pal and he wanted to milk the occasion. Harry had a sign over his desk that read, SUCK IT UP, one that he had started to ignore. He just couldn't suck it up anymore. But he did, one more time, and agreed to go down the street to the Mexican place that was still open and have a beer. Travis had an open Corniche waiting. He paid the attendant a few dollars to keep watching it, and then the girls came pouring out of the Troubadour. They had their hair chopped off and slanted six different ways to nowhere, and their clothes were black and netted and expensively forlorn, but it was them, all right, the same gang that had stopped him cold years back when he first came out to Hollywood and thought he was the only one ever to get a fruit bowl sent up to his room at the Wilshire. As usual, they were mismatched with pale men carrying attaché cases, but they were the cream and they had the kind of undeniable beauty that you simply couldn't be casual about no matter who you were and what coast you were from. He looked around and quite frankly couldn't spot a single one who'd be incapable of slipping past that fence he'd built around himself when he first met Julie— so as not to mess things up. All it would take was the inclination.

"Oh, Jesus Christ," said Harry. "Will you just look at them."

"I can't," said Travis, with a pop singer's heartbreak in his voice. "It's too painful."

"For Christ's sake," said Harry. "Show them the Corniche. You can get laid just on that."

Travis had his first laugh of the evening, and Harry put an arm around his friend's shoulders. Travis put an arm around Harry Towns's waist. A famous first and fuck the sentimentality. They just stood there marveling at the girls, and Harry asked his friend what he would say to fifty thousand.

"Where do I send it?" asked Travis.

"Hey, that's right," said Harry. "You don't even have my address."

They stayed fixed on the girls, watching them dance in place as they waited for their cars, some of them using the Troubadour's awning poles as a ballet bar. Harry knew that there were still some adventures up ahead.

"Oh, yeah," he could hear a friend in the theater say. "Blindness, impotence. I can hardly wait." But that was his friend in the theater. It wasn't Harry Towns. Take the next morning, for example. He'd get up, have a full breakfast, check the trades, then fly back to his family and get set to see what it was like on the receiving end.

Two

〰〰 HE WAS DETERMINED TO SEE *CATS* THIS time. Everybody else had seen it, so why not Harry. Or maybe he would see the new Doc Simon. He had not seen a Simon in ten years. Maybe the man had come up with something. What did he have against Doc Simon?

He would use either *Cats* or the new Simon as a means of getting back to the theater. Then maybe he would see a ballet or try one of the new Thai restaurants. Instead of letting the whole city go to waste.

He thought of this on a Thursday, the night before he was scheduled to go in. But already the pressure of the visit was starting to get to him. He tried out the idea on Julie, who was reading a mystery next to the fireplace. She sat at the other end of the large living room that they had once wanted to design as the lobby of a small rooming house, with bachelor friends sitting in cozy little sections of their own. They had more or less pulled it off, except for inviting the bachelor friends out. They had cordoned themselves off.

"I think I'll see *Cats* this time," he said to her. "Instead of just pissing away the whole evening."

"That's a good idea," she said.

But anything he came up with would have been a good idea. She just wanted to finish the mystery. So she could start a new one. He didn't see how anyone could read that many mysteries—or that so many were published, for that matter. It occurred to him that she might be skipping, but he had only caught her doing that once. They had a neighbor she kept exchanging them with.

17

"Maybe I'll call Hans," he said, mentioning a responsible new friend. "Maybe we'll see it together."

"All right," said Julie, "but you'd better hurry up if you want to catch him in."

Hans was in the wholesale jewelry business. He was the same age as Harry and had his identical hairline. But in spite of his having these qualities, Harry decided he did not feel like seeing *Cats* with him. If Harry had to see it, he would just as soon see it alone.

Megan had fallen asleep in the den, which meant that Harry had a clean shot at the news. As much as he adored his daughter and still couldn't get over the fact that he had one, he was also a little relieved when he didn't have to play with her. He had been down that road before. Not that there weren't certain things he liked doing with her. For example, he had had an enjoyable time taking her class to the police station.

Dan Rather's lead story was a long one on arms control. So Harry figured he might as well get up and make his hotel reservation. Not that he had anything against arms control. There was a chance that he might even chain himself to a facility some day. On behalf of Megan's generation. It just wasn't Harry's idea of a lead story. He felt it should be deeper in.

Harry made the reservation at an out-of-the-way hotel that only a few major film stars stayed at. When people asked if he kept an apartment in the city, he said no. What he had was an arrangement with a hotel. And he did. The arrangement was that if they had a room, they gave it to him, and if they didn't, they would recommend another hotel. And they sent some fruit up to his room. But none of this was important. It was just a drop.

He put a pot pie in the oven and poured himself a Stolichnaya vodka on the rocks. The pot pies came from a woman in the village who insisted they slimmed you down because she refused to put any salt in them. Harry did not see any difference in his waistline, but he liked the pot pies and assumed she knew what she was doing.

THE CURRENT CLIMATE

"You know who else is going to eat one tonight?" she would ask when he had selected his pie. And then she would name an executive at *The New York Times*.

He set the oven at 325 degrees and then called up to get the Dow Jones closing market report. He had bought a hundred shares of a blue-chip stock on Black Monday, mostly to get back at the thirty-year-olds who had made fortunes in the market. But also because he liked the expression *bottom fishing*. He knew it would shock his sister, who lived on Staten Island. He could hear her calling her friends and saying: "Guess what my crazy brother did this time? He went 'bottom fishing.'"

The main thing was to stay focused and not do anything that would jeopardize his plans for the next day. But then he took his first pop of the Stolichnaya vodka and felt his resolve start to fade. Maybe if he just called Nunzi, to see if he was in. It didn't mean he would have to go by and see him. But he would have another option. In case he changed his mind and decided he didn't want to see *Cats* after all. Or let's say he couldn't get a ticket. Who said you could just walk up to the box office at the last minute and get one. He wouldn't even have to speak to Nunzi. The man was used to getting that type of call. Where someone just listened for a second and hung up. It wasn't as if he would go to pieces. Or that Harry was doing something shitty.

On the other hand, who was he kidding. You didn't call Nunzi out of curiosity. To check on his health. And you certainly didn't call him when you were planning to see *Cats* in what was starting to shape up as a pathetic attempt to get the city back.

Julie saved his ass by suggesting that he carry Megan up to her bed. She had been working for the post office when he met her and had suffered a back injury on the job. Some postal workers had tested Julie by heaving hundred-pound bags of mail at her to see if she was strong enough for the work.

"Let's see how you do, little sister" is what one of them had said.

And she had done fine, except for the back injury. Harry had gotten friendly with a dying novelist who used the word *brave* a

19

lot. Skiers were brave. People like that. No doubt it was an out-
dated way of thinking about women, but he always thought of Julie
as being brave for catching the sacks. And he would like to get his
hands on the cocksucker who threw them at her.

Maybe there was something for Goldie Hawn in Julie's days at
the post office.

He scooped up Megan gently, sliding one hand under her as if
it was a spatula and he was trying to flip an egg without breaking
it. A thing he noticed about little girls is that they liked to flap their
arms back and close their eyes—so that they could be ready to be
carried off by a prince or Baryshnikov. So you had to test them
to make sure they were really sleeping. He carried her upstairs and
was fairly certain she was out, although she had fooled him a
couple of times. As he slipped her into bed and pulled her dress
down over her legs, he had to remember not to be lascivious. It
didn't really work that way with a daughter, but he had a feeling
that Julie had been watching him on that count for a while. She
had stopped, however, and may even have been a little disappointed that he had tilted too far the other way.

After he tucked in Megan and turned on her merry-go-round
night-light, he went into the bedroom and got a head start on
packing. That meant making sure he had his vals. They were
important in case he changed his mind about *Cats* and decided to
have that other kind of evening. He also tossed in a few items he
forgot sometimes, such as pine-tar shampoo and throwaway blades.
All he would have to do the next morning was top off these items
with socks and underwear and he would be on his way.

He went downstairs and saw that Julie was now watching a
sitcom to go with her mystery. It had started out with her having
a favorite lineup on Thursday nights. But now she had a whole
week's worth of favorite lineups. Not that he minded that much.
He enjoyed living with a woman who could shift for herself. When
Matty, who was Harry's producer friend, met Julie, he said: "This
one does not need you." He had known some of Harry's girlfriends
and was right on target with this comment. Harry had seen Matty

reach across a table and pinch the nipple of his accountant's girlfriend. He certainly hoped Matty never did that to Julie, since it would end their friendship and Harry would probably have to take a swing at him, a prospect Harry didn't relish, since Matty had done some boxing. He had seen him demonstrate some moves in an elevator, right after two black people got out.

Harry kissed Julie on the back of the neck, which she acknowledged by pushing her head back against him while at the same time keeping her eye on the screen. He poured a second Stolichnaya vodka on the rocks and ate his pot pie at the kitchen table, leaving a small wedge of it so that technically he could not be accused of eating it all. Then he walked out to the shed that he had fixed up as an office. Or, rather, that the previous owner had fixed up before he died. All Harry did was add to it.

The fellow who died had favored sallow colors. Or maybe they had turned sallow after he was in there for a while. Harry had noticed an interior-decorating shop in the village that featured cheery-looking wallpaper selections in the window. He planned to pop in one day and ask the owner—who wore cheery-looking outfits—to come over and see if she could think of a way to make his office cheery. But he wanted to be comfortably out in front before he did that.

The idea of the office was for him to be physically away from the house so that he could be sure to get his work done. But Megan had already discovered where it was, and when Julie came back from the village, she always popped in to use the john, claiming that she couldn't make it to the house. There were days when it seemed the whole family lived in Harry's shed. An alternative would have been to get space in a new office building in the village that had a Colonial facade stuck onto it at the last minute. The developers may have had to stick it on in order to get it approved. An insurance agency had moved in quickly, but no other tenants had followed and the other offices remained empty. Harry thought of renting one right next to the insurance agency so that he would be away from the house during the daytime. Maybe he could strike up a friendship with one of the insurance agents and have lunch with him. But if he was going to do that, he might as well move back to the city.

Harry decided to start a fire in the wood stove. He had once returned from a trip to Los Angeles and found a raccoon in there. It had gotten caught in the stove and hardened up. He was amazed by the ease with which he had plucked it out of there, instead of calling a special person to deal with it. He used that as an example of his excellent adjustment to the country. But he wasn't anxious to find another one in there.

After he lit the fire he took another pop of his Stolichnaya vodka and gave his Spanish Armada play a quick riffle. There was a film and television writers' strike on, and it seemed a perfect time for Harry to see if he could work a little conflict into the piece. So that it wouldn't just be the Spanish and the English fleets facing each other and not doing anything until a storm carried off the Armada. Harry's dying novelist friend who used the word *brave* a lot had said to him: "You're a modest enough fellow, Harry, and that's admirable. But isn't it time to sally out?"

He had accompanied this advice by extending his arm and fluttering two fingers. That may have been why Harry selected the Spanish Armada as a subject . . . as a means of sallying out.

One drawback was that there was very little on the fellow who led the Armada. The Duke of Medina Sedonia owned orange groves in Andalusia and had never been to sea before. Getting more than that was like pulling teeth. But after going through fifty Armada books, Harry had finally spotted a footnote that said the Duke had an interest in an inn called the Six Devils. Harry almost jumped out of his chair when he saw that. It cast a whole new light on the Duke, and there was no question it would help Harry to get some badly needed conflict into the play.

It was getting late, though, and the city was on his mind. You couldn't just shoehorn in a little conflict. And you certainly couldn't do it in one evening. So he put the Armada play back on the shelf. He needed more on the Duke, anyway. And the good stuff was probably in Madrid. If the strike lasted long enough, maybe he would find a way to get over there.

In the meanwhile he drained the rest of the vodka and thought about calling Nunzi to tell him there was a *chance* he might be in the city. And leaving it at that. But he would be taking his life in his hands. If he made a call like that and didn't show up, he would never hear the end of it.

"What the fuck's wrong with you," Nunzi would say, and give him a little slap. "I stayed in all day long and you didn't show."

He was going to be in, anyway, but that was beside the point. You didn't tell Nunzi you *might* show up. You either called him and showed up or you didn't call. In that case, fuck it. He would tough it out. What did Nunzi do, own the city all of a sudden? From his shitty apartment on Northern Boulevard? Harry would go in and eat at a Thai restaurant and see fucking *Cats* if it was the last thing he did on earth. And he did fine with that line of thinking too. He actually got as far as the door before he turned around and picked up the phone.

〜〜 HE DIDN'T GET NUNZI. WHAT HE GOT was Nunzi's machine.

"I am not at home at the moment, dahlinks," went the message, "but if you will be so kind as to leave your name and number, I promise to get back to your face."

He had several accents going in the message, all of which sucked. But at least he had had the good grace not to do his ninth-rate sixties space-cadet bullshit.

"The eye of the eye is the soul of the soul and the key to the universe."

That was the worst. And, incredibly, it had landed him on the payroll of a loopy department-store magnate who had ended up walking the streets of downtown Los Angeles in a bathrobe. Of course, Nunzi had had to get him girls too.

The recorded message meant that Nunzi was probably out of town visiting his straight brother in West Palm. Or maybe he had taken the girl and gone to New Orleans. So they could do the same thing they did in Queens. Sit on their asses in an apartment and blow their brains out. Or maybe go outside and get in an accident. The next time Harry saw Nunzi, he would be all banged up and carrying a cane.

"Cost me ten fucking grand in cash for the doctor, and I'll never walk right again," he would tell Harry.

And then, amazingly, he would heal right up in a week. And some people said he was seventy.

Harry felt betrayed. How could Nunzi just take off like that and leave Harry stranded? Which, of course, was unfair. They had a tacit understanding that Nunzi wasn't supposed to call Harry at home. So what was the man supposed to do, sit on his ass in the apartment with the matador pictures and the fish tank and jerk off while Harry made up his mind if he wanted to honor him with his presence in the city once a month? If he was *lucky,* once a month.

Still, Harry couldn't help it. He felt cut off. Not that he was going to, but what if he changed his mind about *Cats?* What was he supposed to do then? Call Bryan, he guessed, but that meant he would have to hear about Bryan's acting. And get scolded for not coming to see him do *Three Penny Opera* in a toilet on Varick Street. He was the first one to really get the essence of "Mack the Knife." And he would have to smell Bryan's room.

Suddenly Harry's whole plan sounded like shit. Maybe he would just forget the city. Keep his appointment at the medical mall and then turn around and go home. What was he trying to prove with *Cats,* anyway? That he was responsible? That's what you were when you saw *Cats?* Fuck it. He didn't have to see *Cats.* He paid the rent. Nobody missed a meal. He was responsible.

But it was late. Obviously the vodka had thrown off his focus. He would feel differently in the morning. All he had to do was get through to the next day. The second he saw some daylight he would start to love his plan again. He wouldn't even want to *know* Nunzi. He would see that the man had actually done him a favor by being out of town visiting his straight brother in West Palm.

~~ AND HARRY WAS RIGHT. THE NEXT morning he *was* a different person. He didn't even have to see *Cats*. He could do what he wanted to do. Have dinner by himself and just fuck around. See some friends, *don't* see some friends. Enjoy himself.

He knew that he had no chance of making a clean getaway, and sure enough, Julie reached around and grabbed him before he got out of bed. No way was she turning him loose in the city with a full tank. It didn't matter if there was a tornado alert or a delegation from the mayor's office at the front door. He wasn't getting out of there. She rolled her eyes with mock resignation and then disappeared beneath the covers to get him started. When she surfaced, he teased her by saying she used to spend a lot more time under there when they were dating—and she was delivering the mail. She came right back at Harry by saying he was lucky she was under there at all. That women didn't enjoy it all that much. She had checked this with the other moms in the play group. That didn't square with Harry's experience, but who knows, maybe she was on to something. The great thing is that they could have this friendly disagreement while they were making love.

Julie had placed two steaming cups of coffee on the bookshelves, right above their heads. They took sips of it before they got started and drank the rest when they were finished and the coffee had cooled off. Julie asked if he had called Hans or any of his other friends and Harry said no, he wanted to stay loose. Julie knew how to translate this remark—that it involved Nunzi in some way, but she made no comment on the subject.

The one time Nunzi had come out to the house—for the party

they gave when they moved in—his driver had taken the rented limo into a neighbor's pond. And he had grabbed handfuls of Harry's Macanudo cigars and stuffed them into his pockets, as if he were at a benefit. Before the other guests could get a shot at them. Then Harry had to go over to the bed and breakfast and settle Nunzi's bill in cash, since he was not allowed to carry credit cards. So he wasn't exactly a favorite of Julie's. Although when he passed their table at Windows on the World—on one of Julie's rare trips to the city—he was shrewd enough to kiss her hand and say she looked like a Kennedy.

After Harry had showered and dressed, he kissed Julie and hugged Megan, telling her he would bring her a special city toy. She said she had enough toys and could he please stay home. As if he were on the road all the time. He stood there and looked at the ceiling, with Megan pulling at his pants, until Julie shooed him off, saying: "Just go. It'll be fine once you go."

He walked outside and flung his suitcase into the backseat of the Olds. Why did he have to have his fucking heart broken every time he walked out the door? Even when he went to the toolshed. What about people who went to a real office every day? At least he was home most of the time. Although maybe that's why Megan took the trips so hard.

Before he got started, he stood off and checked the car, deciding once again that it looked fine. When the Cadillac broke down, he had decided to replace it with an Olds in order to save a few dollars. Sure enough, Julie's brother had looked at it and said: "I see you went one down."

What a shitty thing for an otherwise great guy to say. But he had not been the same since the diabetes.

Harry looked at his watch and saw that he had better get going if he wanted to catch Ziffren at the medical mall. Ziffren was a psychiatrist Harry had been seeing for twenty-five years. Naturally he was embarrassed about this. He had broken away for about seven—and that was the correct phrase, too—but then Ziffren had written him a letter saying how much he enjoyed not being able to get in to see one of Harry's movies. And how much humanity he had found on the screen once he did get in. He was convinced it was this quality that accounted for the healthy grosses.

They had lunch together in an Italian restaurant, and next thing Harry knew, he was back in treatment. He wasn't even sure why. Ziffren had probably spotted something at the lunch. Still, Harry figured if he got at least one good notion out of each visit, it was worth it. And he did. For example, Ziffren had told him that sometimes the best way to handle a situation was to do nothing. That had never occurred to Harry before. He always had to do something. Ziffren also pointed out that it was all right to lie. Not every two seconds, but once in a while. Harry hadn't realized that, either. So there were two right there—doing nothing and lying.

Ziffren's office was right on the way to the city, so he didn't have to drive too far out of his way for the visits. Still, he planned to break away the first chance he got. He didn't want to go right through with Ziffren holding his hand. It was as if the whole thing might not count.

Harry stopped off at the deli to pick up one of their great egg sandwiches and a double cup of dark coffee with no sugar. After eight years he was allowed to go behind the counter and pour his own. He still couldn't use the john, but that would follow. Then he went across the road to the stationery store to pick up the newspapers and two cigars. Even though Harry bought two of them a day, Van did not automatically hand them over. Harry had to say: "And I'll take two cigars." Van did not want to give off the slightest impression that he condoned cigar smoking.

Harry cut a triangular notch in the lid of the coffee container for easy sipping and arranged the sandwich in his lap so that he could take bites of it while he was driving. Then he took off, slowing down when he passed The Mansione to see if there was any sign that Fielding had made it up from Boca Raton. When Harry had first moved into the highly conservative community, he had expected to be cut a lot. He was prepared for it, and when it didn't happen, he relaxed a bit and told himself it was a different world. And then Fielding cut him. Harry had volunteered his house for a property association meeting, setting up a buffet table and a bar. Then Fielding, a handsome, silver-haired man, barged in with a sheaf of documents and said: "We've got a lot of work to do," knocking a few of Harry's chopped chicken liver hors d'oeuvres off the table. Then he took over the meeting while Harry sat there steaming.

"I am finished now," Fielding said after his presentation, "and prepared to hear what anyone else has to say."

Most of the people were old-timers, half of whom could not hear. Harry got up and made a little speech in which he said he regarded the little community as more than property. That there were some remarkable people in the room and it was no accident that they were all drawn to the same little area. He wasn't even sure he meant this. From what he had seen, the only thing that mattered to the group was land values, and these people would cut your throat over a blade of grass. But he wanted to show that he was above such considerations. He felt that he had evened the score with Fielding. They were both rough-and-tumble types who had each gotten in one. They could now proceed to live in the community, not necessarily as friends, but begrudgingly respectful of one another. And then Fielding cut him again. Harry had nipped inside to catch the score of the Giants' football game and then come back to report it to Fielding.

"I know the score," Fielding said with a thin smile.

It wasn't what he said but the way he said it. Then he left and everyone followed him, none of them stopping at the buffet table. Harry and Julie had to eat the hors d'oeuvres themselves over the next few nights.

And so Harry, with a weird sense of relief, felt he finally had an enemy in the community. But it was pretty tepid stuff. Not like the good old days when they came right out and called you a kike. And then, soon afterward, he saw Fielding, with a cane and dark glasses, being led into the post office. And later in the day he saw him again, being brought down to the lake, as if to get a last look at it. They took him down to his winter home in Boca and there was some question as to whether he would ever make it up again. Considering the cuts, you might think that Harry would be pulling for Fielding to drop dead in Boca. So that another kind of couple could move in. But Harry could not get himself to feel that way. Not that he wished him a speedy recovery. He just didn't give a shit about him. He did wonder about The Mansione, though. A Secretary of Commerce had once been married in it. Could they unload it? What price would it bring? It seemed to Harry that only someone who owned discos would know what to do with it.

Harry had the hour-and-a-half trip timed out to within five minutes. He could afford to be more leisurely, since Nunzi was out of town and he did not have to stop at the bank. When the new accountant asked him about the large monthly cash withdrawals, Harry had told her he dealt with some funny people. Hadn't the accountant seen his movies? These people needed to be paid in cash. "A-ha," said the accountant over the phone, as if she now had all the ammunition she needed. And she could hardly wait to be questioned about the withdrawals so she could tell the agent about the funny people Harry dealt with.

Harry filled in the driving time by trying to learn Italian again. It was the kind of cassette where they just threw you in without any English translation. He felt he had been thrown in too fast. So far it was just a bunch of Italian to him. But maybe it would click in one day, and all of a sudden he would be speaking Italian.

As he drove into the parking lot of the medical mall, he thought about the first time he had gone to see Ziffren. He and Sally had turned up together to see if they could save the marriage. She was having an affair with an Israeli, but she had agreed to see Ziffren, anyway. One of the things that came up was Sally's frigidity. Or at least her unwillingness to sleep with Harry.

"What's the big deal," said Ziffren. "You just lie back and spread your legs."

Even Harry had winced at that, and after a few sessions Sally had stormed out. Except for a quick visit in which she had tried to get Ziffren's approval of the Israeli, she had never come back. Who knows, maybe Ziffren had blown the marriage. Not that there was that much to blow. Harry had hung in there with Ziffren, and in the years that followed, they had both changed along with the culture. Ziffren saying spread your legs before anyone knew about women, then setting up a date for Harry with a Swedish researcher at the time when sex was freewheeling. Later he became sensitive to women and insisted his wife become a psychiatrist, too, in the office next to his. And now, in the current climate, he warned Harry to be careful about hookers.

When Harry walked in, Ziffren was standing in the middle of his office and seemed to be trying out his legs after some recent surgery. Harry had asked him about the procedure—in case he had to have one of his own—and Ziffren had assured him it was routine. But Harry noticed that when he sat down, he crossed and recrossed his legs like a woman. So it could not have been a walk in the park.

Harry told Ziffren how nicely he was getting along and how well he was bearing up under what was turning out to be a harsh and bitter strike. He was tempted to mention the anonymous letter that had come in, calling Harry a scab; it had been taken seriously, causing Harry enormous pain. But he decided to keep the visit short and sweet. It was a bright and clear day. Nunzi was away in West Palm, and Harry just wanted to get back on the road so that he could begin to enjoy the city in a normal way.

In spite of his need to get moving, he found that he was unable to take his eyes off Ziffren's hair. Harry was aware that the psychiatrist had a full head of it, but never before had it looked so beautiful to him. It was exactly the kind that Harry wanted, gray, but not the kind that was a minus. Harry had spent a tremendous amount of time wondering if he should dye his own hair and had always backed off at the last minute.

"I would lose a little something," he had told Julie, who felt it looked fine the way it was.

31

But if Harry could get his hair the same color as Ziffren's, there was no doubt in his mind that he would jump in and have it dyed.

"I can't help but notice how great your hair looks," he told Ziffren. "Did you do something to it?"

"Thank you," said Ziffren, running his palms along the sides. "I just had it done this morning."

He said he had it worked on once a month, but Harry probably hadn't noticed it before because you had to catch it right after the treatment.

"If you like," said Ziffren, who was aware that Harry was ashamed of his own hair, "I'll get you an appointment with my colorist. You can see him on the same days that you see me.

"Or better yet," he said, grabbing at the edge of the desk and getting to his feet with some effort, "I'll take you over and introduce you to Ron right now."

As much as Harry admired Ziffren's hair, he was not sure he wanted to get involved with his colorist. Harry's objective, after all, was to break away for good. And it seemed to him that going to Ziffren's colorist would only tie him in tighter. On the other hand, there was probably no harm in meeting the colorist and getting an opinion. Was it possible to get his kind of hair the same shade as Ziffren's? Also, it would get him out of the office and effectively end the visit.

The salon was a few streets away from the medical mall. Ziffren was still a little shaky on his feet, and Harry was tempted to offer him his arm for support. But he had tried that once with his aging father, who had smacked it away. So he was careful about offering his arm to people.

"The trick is to get the right man," said Ziffren as they crossed the parking lot. "And Ron is the best."

To show that he was in accordance with Ziffren's thinking, Harry said that was true of many professions.

"There are a few good actors, a few good writers, a few good everything."

"Exactly," said Ziffren.

THE CURRENT CLIMATE

There were no customers in the salon when they arrived, which surprised Harry since it was lunch hour and it seemed a perfect time for executives in the area to have their hair colored. Ziffren introduced Harry to a slim young man with an open shirt whose own hair was indeterminate in color, as if he hadn't decided which way to go with it.

"Ron," said Ziffren, "this is a patient of mine who is interested in having his hair colored."

Then he sat down in the reception area to let the two men work out their own arrangements. Harry was surprised that Ziffren had unmasked him as a patient, but he forgave him since he still seemed a little befuddled after his recent procedure.

"You're a *patient?*" said Ron, who acted as if it were the funniest thing he had ever heard.

"Just once a month," said Harry.

"Once a *month,*" said Ron.

Harry couldn't tell if Ron felt he was seeing Ziffren too often or not often enough.

"It gets me by," said Harry.

"I'll bet it does," said Ron significantly. Then he stood off a bit for a look at Harry's hair.

"Oh *yeah,*" he said, moving closer and giving it a gentle pull. "I'd *love* to do it. Do you want to make an appointment?"

"I'm not absolutely sure I want to go forward yet," said Harry.

"Just browsing, huh," said Ron despondently.

His moods seemed to flash back and forth between the Comic and the Tragic, as if he were wearing one of the masks that hung in theater lobbies.

"Why make an appointment and not keep it," said Harry.

"I see what you mean," said Ron, still in the Tragic mode.

A thumping sound came from the reception area. Harry had assumed that Ziffren was dozing, but he had evidently slipped off the chair and now lay sprawled on the floor.

Harry ran to his side, with Ron following close behind.

"Jesus Christ," said Ron, his eyes bright and mischievous, as if he were a boy who had discovered a treasure. "Do you think he fainted?"

"I think so," said Harry, whose father had been a fainter as well.

"Should we move him?" asked Ron.

Harry felt it was a toss-up. He seemed to recall that you weren't supposed to move fainters. On the other hand, if they waited for help, they might lose him. They were close to the medical mall, but there were all those exposés about bungled emergency calls.

"Do you know CPR?" he asked Ron.

Harry had once organized a course in the technique for his immediate neighbors, hiring a nurse to teach it. But at the last minute he had been called to L.A. on a rewrite and did not get to attend it himself.

"Me?" said Ron, putting a hand to his chest. "Shit, no."

"Then let's move him."

Harry got the psychiatrist under the arms, and Ron took his legs. Apart from a few hugs in the freewheeling seventies, it was the first time he had ever had physical contact with Ziffren.

"Fucker weighs a ton," said Ron as they carried him across the parking lot.

"That's because he fainted," said Harry.

"You're right," said Ron, in a return to seriousness.

By the time they got him back to his office, Ziffren had started to revive. Harry wondered if it was a Freudian faint, brought on, as an example, by a last-minute conflict over whether to share his colorist with Harry. Hadn't Freud fainted when he was at the seashore with Breur or someone like that?

"Keep an eye on him," he told Ron, and then ran next door in the hope of summoning Ziffren's wife. He didn't know much about Tess Ziffren, although he may have caught a glimpse of her at a carnival. Psychiatry seemed to be a case of I-show-you-mine and I-never-get-to-see-yours.

Tess Ziffren turned out to be a short, buxom woman who gave

off an aura of great authority. She wore a tailored suit and a string of pearls and had been talking to a fat girl.

When Harry broke in, she rose to her full height and said: "Now look here. I demand an explanation."

"I'm sorry," said Harry. "I'm a long-term patient of your husband's. He seems to have fainted at the hair colorist."

"Oh, my God," said Tess Ziffren, shuddering with horror.

"Excuse me, darling," she said to the fat girl, and ran next door to the adjoining office.

"Are you all right, Stu?" she asked, kneeling at her husband's side.

"I'm fine, baby," said Ziffren, who seemed amused by the episode. "I seem to have fainted. But I don't want to talk about it because that in itself might trigger another fainting spell."

He said there was a name for the syndrome but he couldn't think of it at the moment. "I'm sure it will come to me," he said.

"We thought we'd better bring him over here," said Ron proudly.

Mrs. Ziffren looked at Ron with disapproval and then made a phone call for help. After listening to the voice at the other end of the line, she broke in and said: "I want someone over here right now."

She hung up the phone and took some cheese and crackers from Ziffren's mini-refrigerator. Oddly flirtatious, she threw out a hip and asked: "Would you boys like a snack?"

"No thanks," said Harry, although he was beginning to develop an appetite. Ron just held up a hand and blushed.

Two attendants arrived with a gurney.

"You see now it pays to work here," said Ziffren.

"Is there anything I can do?" asked Harry as the psychiatrist was lifted onto the vehicle.

"It doesn't appear so," said Ziffren.

His wife covered him with a blanket and told him not to exert himself.

35

"Then I'll just keep my fingers crossed," said Harry, "and hope it works out all right."

"Hey," said Ron. "I will too."

Ziffren told the attendants to just hold it for a moment while he explained to Harry that he didn't dismiss such gestures as meaningless and was doing research on the scientific underpinnings of superstition.

"But I don't want to get into that now," said Ziffren.

Ziffren signaled the attendants that it was all right to proceed. He was then wheeled off, with Tess Ziffren walking majestically behind him. At the end of the corridor, he sat up and waved courageously, in a gesture that was reminiscent of FDR.

"Bitch is probably thrilled," said Ron when the Ziffrens were out of view.

"She seems legitimately concerned," said Harry.

"Hey, listen," said Ron, switching attitudes. "Tess Ziffren is a wonderful woman."

He shoved his hands in his pockets and pawed at the ground as if he were about to begin a dance number. Then he raised his eyes and asked Harry if he wanted to go ahead with the rinse.

"Let's find out how he is first," said Harry.

"We probably should," said Ron, crestfallen again.

"But, listen," he said, brightening. "It was great meeting you. And don't worry about the appointment. I'm making plenty of money on my paintings."

〰〰 IT WAS ONLY WHEN HARRY GOT BACK on the highway that the full impact of Ziffren's situation hit him. What if he lost his old friend? Who would he run to if someone killed his ass in tennis? On a more serious note, what if he lost Megan, the cornerstone of his life, even though he didn't play with her enough? Or what if Harry himself came up with a spot on the lung? It had happened to his last accountant, who also played tennis and smoked cigars. Harry hadn't discussed death with Ziffren, assuming they would get to it at the proper time. The psychiatrist was an expert on the subject and was often called upon to lecture on it at the Coast Guard Academy.

On the positive side, if Ziffren passed on, Harry would finally be finished with him. How would he handle his life? Probably the same way other people did, feel miserable and muddle through. Did Donald Trump dance away the days? In an emergency, there were others Harry could consult, Julie being a case in point. Though she was normally preoccupied and he practically had to make an appointment to get her full attention, he felt confident he could rely on her in the clutch. She always listened to him in restaurants. Nor did it stop with his wife. He had met a fascinating psychiatrist at an art show in Los Angeles. Harry had always been struck by the fact that the Nazis kept a psychoanalytic institute going during the war. He posed a question to this man. What would a doctor tell an SS man, for example, who was troubled by killing Jew after Jew?

"Try a Gypsy," the psychiatrist had said without missing a beat.

37

What was wrong with this man, even though Harry would have to move to the Coast to see him on a regular basis.

Not once, as Harry continued along to the city, did he stop to consider what Ziffren was going through and that he was probably scared shit about fainting again and possibly dropping dead altogether. The fact that he ignored Ziffren's condition probably meant that after twenty-five years he needed a few more sessions with him. If Harry had been a decent man with a healthy outlook on life, he would at least have given a thought to the plight of his old friend. But Harry put Ziffren out of his mind. He felt confident that Ziffren would want him to go ahead and try to have a normal time in the city.

Once again Harry got excited when he saw the skyline. That was usually it; he saw the skyline, called Nunzi, and it was case closed. But since Nunzi was in West Palm, he had a chance to really enjoy himself this time, and even partake of the city's cultural wonders. *Cats* had never been a serious possibility, but why not a Lorca play? He'd always had an appointment with Lorca. Now would be a good time to keep it. Or maybe he could check out the old Jews on the Lower East Side. He had heard there was a store that was entirely thrown over to yarmulkes. He could visit that store. Normally Harry only went to museums in other cities, but maybe he would try one on this visit. He hadn't seen the dinosaurs in a long time and he had always loved them. He wouldn't have to spend a lot of time there, just see a few dinosaurs and get out. Or maybe he would just wander around and strike up conversations with girls in front of water fountains. If he happened to pick one off, fine—if not, no problem. He got dizzy thinking of all the possibilities that lay ahead of him. At one time he thought it was too late, that he had blown a decade. But he had kissed a young girl at midnight outside of Nicky Blair's restaurant in Los Angeles and she hadn't said a word about his gray hair.

〜〜 EVEN THOUGH A SMALL FORTUNE HAD been spent refurbishing it, Harry's hotel still had a musty smell to it. A poetical explanation would have been that all the sordid dramas enacted within its rooms had entered the beams. But a more likely one was that the only way to eliminate mustiness was to start over. As he walked across the lobby, the aging Hispanic bellboys, one by one, said, "Welcome home, Mr. Towns," which embarrassed Harry and seemed to annoy a man in a striped suit who had entered the hotel at the same time as Harry and did not get the same greeting.

"Who the hell are you?" asked the man, matching him step for step as they crossed the lobby.

"I'm an old customer," said Harry, wondering immediately if he should have been sharper. Who the fuck are *you?* is what he should have said.

Harry approached the concierge's desk and asked to have a VCR sent up to his room. This was in case he got the urge to watch a couple of porno flicks late in the evening. Which he probably would, even though he planned to spend a normal day in the city. The concierge said that Kiss had the only VCR and that there was some question as to whether the group would be checking out that day. He was filling in for the real concierge, who was out sick. Clearly it meant a great deal to him that Kiss was in the hotel. Harry felt that the real concierge would have taken Kiss in stride. He told the temporary concierge to see what he could do and slipped him ten dollars. But as he approached the front desk, Harry realized that the whole question of whether he would have a VCR in his room had been left up in the air.

The manager of the hotel, a genial young Frenchman with a yellow carnation in his lapel, spotted Harry and greeted him with a big wink, one boulevardier to another. Even though he had no evidence that Harry was a boulevardier. Although the manager's greeting had been warm, there was a small trace of hurt in his expression, no doubt having to do with the restaurant. Harry could see it over the manager's shoulder. It was not doing well despite the captain's brisk efforts to create a different impression. The manager had been given instructions by the Canadians to push it and could not understand why someone like Harry did not help out.

"I never see you in our restaurant," said the manager. "How come?"

"Someone always takes me out to dinner," said Harry lamely.

Actually he had tried the restaurant once and found the food insipid, although he had to concede it was arranged artistically.

"Why can't they take you here," said the manager. "They're going to go crazy over the food.

"And then," he said, touching Harry's arm and giving him another wink, "maybe we'll do something together."

This last was no doubt in reference to the lingerie shows he was known to stage in his personal suite. But first Harry would have to eat a few meals in the restaurant.

The young man behind the desk gave Harry a registration form. He had an English accent and may or may not have been English. He also had a general awareness that Harry was in the entertainment business.

"Anything coming up?" he asked as Harry filled out the form.

Harry told him about the dog show, which didn't seem to interest him.

"Anything else?" asked the clerk.

Straining a bit, Harry mentioned a concept he was working on that was being kicked around at Orion as a possibility for Cher.

"Oh," said the clerk, perking up. "When will it be out?"

THE CURRENT CLIMATE

"These things take time," said Harry, unable to control his irritation. "You just don't rush them into theaters."

"Oh, well," said the clerk, clearly displeased. "You're in 618."

Harry took his own bag up to the room and unpacked, double-checking to make sure he had brought along his vals. Then he saw to it that the door to the adjoining room was secure. The hotel was lax about such matters; on one occasion a Brazilian couple had strolled in and caught him reading *Juggs*.

He called Julie and told her he had made it into the city all right. She asked if he had set up a dinner date with Hans or one of his other friends, and Harry said no and told her about Ziffren.

"He'll be just fine," she said, but she was out of breath and distracted and was just saying that. He said he would call her later on.

"No mention of this morning's love?" she asked before hanging up.

"I loved it," he said.

Then he went downstairs to pick up a bottle of Stolichnaya vodka and some porno flicks. On the way out of the hotel he passed the concierge, who said that Kiss hadn't made up its mind yet about checking out.

"How does it look?" asked Harry.

He didn't want to be up there at four in the morning with porno flicks and no VCR to put them on.

"We're doing everything we can," said the concierge.

At the video shop, Harry looked for the Puerto Rican girl who could always be counted on for a few recommendations. He still couldn't get over the fact that she knew exactly the kind he liked, ones with attractive women and a lot of teasing. In his eyes, this transformed her from an ordinary-looking person into a fascinating individual. After all, she had to watch the tapes in order to know which ones Harry would like. But it seemed to be her day off. The clerk was a teenage boy with bad skin. Harry was not anxious to know his recommendations so he proceeded to pick out his own.

41

The ones he chose all had to do with blondes—*Better Blondes, The Best of Blondes,* and *Blonde Explosion.* As he paid the rental fee, he realized that he may have seen *Better Blondes,* but he recalled a sequence in it that he liked and decided to take it along, anyway. He had some porno tapes of his own, but when Megan was born, he had stuffed them into a chest in his office. He just couldn't see having his tapes on the same VCR as *Donald Duck Presents,* although he realized that that's the way life was. Besides, he didn't really have any urge to see porno tapes in the country.

When he got back to the room, the VCR still wasn't there. He had planned to take a quick look at the tapes before he got started, so he was a little disappointed. He sat on the bed and looked at the labels to see who was in them. But he could not seem to get untracked. The yarmulke store was all the way downtown on the Lower East Side; suddenly it seemed a long way to go to see a store that had placed such a limitation on its merchandise.

What do you really want to do? he asked himself. Harry did a great many things in life reflexively. Or because someone else had decided that he should do them. This seemed like a good time to break the habit. He decided that what he really wanted to do most was call a hand model who had led him to believe that she would welcome such a call. She had turned up on the same bus as Harry, who rarely took buses, and Harry had decided it was no accident. He was on his way to have some root-canal work done, so nothing had come of it at the time. But it might now. The trouble was that the hand model knew Julie, and if they wound up rolling around together it would ultimately make him feel like shit. Besides, he wasn't one hundred percent sure about the bus ride. So that was the end of the hand model.

Having eliminated her, the next choice was easy. What he really wanted to do was eat some old-fashioned Chinese food, which he could not get in the country. He knew a place within walking distance of the hotel where the egg rolls were so crisp, you could hear it across the street when someone bit into one. He would get two of them and some sliced pork that he could trust for a change.

THE CURRENT CLIMATE

Maybe throw in some chicken wings. He would eat this at the bar alongside some horse players who would probably eye him with suspicion at first. But once they overheard his small talk to the bartender, they would see that he was all right and include him in their group. He would have to tear himself away from them. And he would take it from there. What a great idea, he told himself. He practically bounded out of bed and got his coat. But then he called Nunzi. And this time Nunzi answered the phone.

〰〰 WHY, OH WHY DID HE HAVE TO MAKE
that call. When he was almost safely out the door. There
went his dream of having a normal day in the city. And
it would take him three days to get over the kind of day
he would now have to have. He could say good-bye to the
Chinese food too. Now that he knew Nunzi was home, it
was important to get over there. Even Nunzi left the apartment
sometimes.

Harry had been startled when Nunzi picked up the phone, and
a little upset. But he had called him, hadn't he? So he must have
wanted to find him in.

Nunzi had sounded like death warmed over. He was probably
smoking a cigarette, and his face no doubt was twice its normal
size. As the day wore on, it would come back down, and he would
look pretty good, a little bit like Sinatra, whose moves he may have
studied. He had asked if Harry was in the city, and for a second
Harry had hesitated. But where else was he supposed to be? Nunzi
had told him to get his ass over there. He and the girl had just come
up from Boca. And they would love to see Harry.

The first thing he had to do was get some money. He cashed a
check for a bill at the desk—it was their limit—and then walked
over to the Hilton and got five hundred from American Express.
That would cover him with Nunzi, and he would have enough left
over in case he decided to get crazy. If for some reason he decided
not to, he would be able to use the cash to buy Megan a dress that
was made in Provence or someplace like that. The kind you could
only find in the city. And he would still have enough walking-
around money to last him for a month in the village, where you

44

couldn't really spend anything. But only once or twice had he made it back home with the cash.

On the way to the bridge he passed the theater where *Cats* was playing. There were only a few people at the box office, and the surrounding neighborhood looked grim and unattractive in the daylight. But all that would change in the evening. There would be people spilling out onto the sidewalk. He felt a little twinge of regret about not getting to see the show and had to keep reminding himself that it only had the one song.

He slipped the doorman at Nunzi's building two dollars. In return, the doorman waved him through and then called upstairs to say that Harry was on his way. Instead of making Harry wait there at the door. He was annoyed that he had started giving him two dollars for this service and on occasion cut him back to one.

On the elevator he met an old-timer with a shopping bag who had played a salesman in one of Harry's first pictures. He reminded the man of this. For a moment the old-timer seemed to recall the experience. He straightened right up. But then the recollection faded. Nonetheless, when the elevator stopped at his floor, he held the door for a moment and said, "Say hi to all the gang." Then he got out.

Harry wondered how he got along. Who took care of him? Could he look after himself with a shattered memory? It was the first time Harry had ever met anyone he knew in Nunzi's elevator.

When he came to the twelfth floor, Harry walked down the hall and stopped at the familiar door marked 12-M. He had once thought of setting a film in the apartment and calling it *12-M.* Or maybe a play. He mentioned this to Nunzi, who quickly forgot it was Harry's idea. From time to time he would say to Harry: "How about a movie called *12-M?*" But Harry didn't get into it with him.

The former child star opened the door. He was wearing an undershirt and big BVDs and had probably overslept and missed out on another job. He had either come down from upstate or flown in from California. But one way or another, he had overslept and missed out on a job. To someone who couldn't shine his shoes. The

45

actor let Harry in and then curled up on Nunzi's couch and went back to sleep.

Nunzi was trying on a jacket while a pale and heavily perspiring man stood by with a tape measure. The jacket came down below his crotch, and although Harry could see the edge of his tiny buns, he could not tell if Nunzi was wearing underwear. The old man, who was Nunzi's friend, and some kind of associate, sat in a chair, examining his manicured nails. He wore a beret and had soft, powerful shoulders. He was rumored to be seventy-six years old and had spent most of his life in prison. But he had a forest of curls and looked twenty years younger, so in a sense the years in prison had been kind to him.

"Say hello to Harry," Nunzi told the old man who had met Harry several times before. "He is a genius, but they keep fucking him."

Nunzi had once seen a picture in which Harry had had to share the credit with a husband-and-wife comedy team. He took that as evidence that Harry was always being mistreated by the industry. In that particular case he had not been far wrong.

"What percentage do you get?" asked Nunzi.

Harry told him he normally got five percent of the net profits on a picture, but that the figure was meaningless since there were a thousand ways to define what a percentage point meant.

"They stay awake all night figuring out ways not to pay you," said Harry.

Nunzi nodded as if he saw what Harry meant. But Harry could tell that as far as Nunzi was concerned, five percent meant five percent, and that was the end of it. Maybe at one time it had been that way.

The old man went into a generalized murder story, entering in the middle as if he had begun it earlier, perhaps in another location. It had to do with the difficulty of making collections and his failure to throw a man out of the window of an office building.

"You can't do that anymore," he said with a sigh, recalling a sunnier time. "That's murder one."

THE CURRENT CLIMATE

"So what do you think, Harry?" asked Nunzi, holding his trim little body erect and shooting imaginary cuffs. He had wonderful posture.

Harry said the jacket looked a little long. He realized this wasn't helpful to the man with the tape measure, but he wasn't worried about him. If he was worried about anyone, he was worried about the old man who could erupt on you. And although the suit had a designer label, the chances were that it had come off a truck.

"A little long," said Nunzi, building on Harry's comment. "Fuckin' jacket's down to my ankles."

"I'll fix it," said the man with the tape measure.

"Fix it," said Nunzi. "You better fuckin' fix it."

But after grumbling a bit he said he would take all six of the suits that the man had brought along. He peeled some bills off a roll and handed them to the man. He was one of the few people Harry knew who still carried a roll.

"Twenty bucks apiece," said Nunzi when the man had left. "And they came off a truck."

He went into the bedroom and reappeared in a green dressing gown with wide, padded shoulders. The former child star sat up and said it was one of Tony Bennett's people in Upstate New York who had caused him to be late for the audition.

"I know that guy," said Nunzi. "He's your best friend, and then all of a sudden he's with Bennett and he don't know you."

"*I want respect,*" Nunzi cried out, balling up his fists and throwing out his jaw.

"Take it easy," said Harry.

He could talk to Nunzi that way at this stage of the evening, although he might not be able to later on.

"Be mature," said the old man, pronouncing it *matoor.*

"You're right," said Nunzi, apologizing to Harry. "I was over-reacting."

"You didn't have any self-esteem," said the old man.

Nunzi went over to the easel and put a few touches on the bullfighter picture. He had been working on the same picture seven

47

years back when Harry first met him. He stood back with the brush raised and asked Harry what he thought of it.

"It's coming along nicely," said Harry.

You were supposed to be in the apartment to admire his artwork.

"I think it needs more orange," said Nunzi, giving it another dab.

"I'm not afraid of anybody," said the old man, as if he were at a job interview.

The girl came out in her slip and lit a cigarette. She was blond and six feet three inches tall and had once run a filling station in West Texas.

"We never go out," she said, her hands shaking. "I want to go somewhere."

"You just got back from fuckin' Boca," said Nunzi. "That's not out?"

"He really understands women," she said, rolling her eyes.

She had a beautiful body, and somehow Harry expected he would have seen more of it by now. But the best he had done up to this point was to see her in the slip.

When the girl went back to the bedroom, Nunzi signaled Harry, who followed him into the kitchen.

"So what can I do you for?" asked Nunzi.

He took the container out of the Rice Krispies box and looked at the wall, bouncing up and down on his toes as if he were at a urinal.

"How about a key?" Harry joked.

He felt it was important for him to let Nunzi know he was familiar with street talk.

"A key," said Nunzi. "I got to know you since childhood for a key."

Harry said he would take two and a half. One was ridiculous, two wouldn't be enough if he had to share it, and three was uncomfortably close to an eighth, which would put him back in an unappealing category. He had given the matter a lot of thought. Nunzi measured off the two and a half on a scale and then sealed it up in a packet, which he handed to Harry without comment. Harry paid him the two-fifty. Once, after handing Harry the dope, he had said, "Here is your medicine," which Harry didn't appreciate. Harry had let the remark go by, but Nunzi, who was not insensitive, had never used it again. They seemed to be a little afraid of each other.

Harry took a seat opposite a framed poster that had been done for the French version of one of his films. He had signed it "To Nunzi, a truly great guy . . . Harry Towns."

Nunzi had put it up on the wall in a prominent position so that everyone who came through his apartment would be sure to see it. Harry had even updated it once, saying that Nunzi was still a great guy and adding the new date. It made him uneasy to look at it; giving it to Nunzi had probably been a mistake. He even thought of asking for it back, but that wouldn't have worked at all. So he just suffered with the lapse of judgment. And what the hell, he figured, I signed it, so I must have meant it.

No one asked him to, but Harry spread some of the dope out on the table, thinking that maybe he should have gotten a little more.

"Thank you, old chap," said the old man, going over to an English accent.

It sounded like a parody of one, except that the old man didn't do parody. Nunzi's ascot, the old man's accent. They had been in prison together and must have concluded that the way to deal with the outside world was with classiness. Harry had met a carpet salesman in the apartment who told him that on Nunzi's first day in prison he had bent over and shown his bony ass to the black population, hollering out: "You want it, come and get it."

No one knew if they had, but the gesture had given him stature.

The former child star got off the couch and joined them at the table, carrying a cup of coffee, some of which spilled out on the rug.

"What the fuck is wrong with you," said Nunzi.

49

He got down on his knees with a napkin and tried to rub out the stains.

"I told you this was an antique."

Nunzi took tremendous pride in his apartment with the Buddhas and the fish tank. And come to think of it, Harry thought, why shouldn't he?

"We go way back together," said the former child star, as if to explain the incident.

He filled Harry in on the illnesses of other former child stars he knew; then he asked Harry to keep him in mind if something came up on the Coast. Harry said he certainly would, although, with the best of intentions, he couldn't think of what kind of roles to keep him in mind for. It was difficult to get a handle on his style.

Harry would not have minded saying good-bye at that point, but he took some of the blow and saw that he was going to be around for a while. You didn't just walk out the door when the old man was around.

"I like an old broad," said the old man, as if it were his turn in a round of such stories. He put out his huge hands as if he were holding such a woman.

"They appreciate it."

His lips were soaked and Harry could see that he would be capable of murder.

Harry said he knew what he meant.

Nunzi disappeared into the bedroom and came back with a diamond ring, which he showed to Harry.

"Twenty-two thousand," said Nunzi. "What do you think?"

The old man leaned forward respectfully to see what Harry thought.

"I don't know much about them," said Harry, which wasn't strictly true, since he had done some research on diamonds along the Houston waterfront. This one was a funny color and was in a dime-store setting.

"It just came off an estate," said Nunzi, holding it up for his own inspection and trying Harry again.

"I don't think so," said Harry.

He was about to tell Nunzi he didn't have that kind of money, anyway. But if he had, Nunzi would have brought up the check. When he first met Nunzi, he had shown him a six-figure residual payment he had received on a picture. It was the biggest one he had ever gotten, although once the taxes were taken out, it went back down under six figures. Harry had been showing off, but at the same time he had felt a need to share his joy with someone. And Nunzi had shared it with him for a while. But then he began to share it less and less. He said that you didn't show unless you shared. Harry waved it off by saying he had pissed it away, anyway. But Nunzi didn't care about that. There were certain things he harped on.

Nunzi let in a short, fat man in a business suit that Harry recognized as having been purchased at Dunhill's. He could tell by the cut. Nunzi told the man to stand in the corner.

"He doesn't want anyone to know he's here," said Nunzi.

"My lips are sealed," said Harry, acting as a spokesman for the group.

"Touché," said the old man.

Having received this assurance, Nunzi gave the man some blow, which he consumed quickly in little rabbity snorts while looking around continually, as if he still weren't convinced his visit would go unreported. He left quickly.

"Wall Street guy," said Nunzi.

"How come everyone is allowed to know I'm here," said Harry, looking ruefully at his movie poster, "and no one is allowed to know about him?"

"Because you're brilliant," said Nunzi, rubbing Harry's head with a knuckle and kissing him on both cheeks. "*Brilliant*. Only you let them fuck you."

Harry felt pacified, although it may have been a result of the dope.

The old man put an arm across his chest, as if he were doing a civilian salute to the flag. Then he released the arm, which flew

51

to the side as if it were operated by a spring. Harry felt that the force of the resulting blow could have cut a tree in half.

"That's in case the chap beside you is facetious," he explained. "Would you like to learn the move?"

Actually Harry would not have minded at all. It seemed to be all you would ever need.

"My card," said the old man, presenting him with one. He had evidently set up a school to teach sudden blows.

"Hey, hey," said Nunzi, running over quickly. "Anything between you two is with me."

"Of course," said Harry, acting offended, as if he didn't have to be told something that obvious.

Nunzi's old friend Marge came up, along with a young woman who just missed out on being beautiful. Normally Harry wouldn't have noticed that she came up short in this area, but she was tall and slender and stylishly dressed, as if she were supposed to be beautiful. And it was your fault if she wasn't. Harry felt it was his responsibility to push her over the edge.

Marge was in her sixties and had the face of a third baseman, but she wore frilly clothes and although Harry couldn't figure it out, he found her appealing. He wasn't exactly ready to roll around with her, but it was not out of the question. Also, no one had asked him. Her hands shook when she took the coke; watching her was like seeing an everyday person, a saleswoman or somebody's aunt, in a porno flick. He would not have wanted to argue this in a panel discussion, but there was something brave about her being an old coker. Not in the manner of the skiers and game hunters that his dying novelist friend wrote about. She was another kind of brave. All of a sudden Harry saw brave women everyplace he looked.

Marge grabbed Nunzi's hair and said, "I love this man."

The woman who was almost beautiful watched her every move. Marge may have been running her.

She said she had written the first three pages of a short story and would Harry like to read it. He said it would be better if he had the entire story in hand. Someone must have told her about him.

"Virginia Woolf is overrated," she said. "So's the whole Bloomsbury group if you ask me."

"It depends on how you look at it," said Harry, who could see that he was going to have trouble fielding her remarks.

"I'm always getting fucked," she said with a sigh.

"Did you hear that, Harry?" said Nunzi, who appeared to be having trouble with her material as well. "She's always getting fucked."

Harry was starting to enjoy himself. There was a writer's bar in Tribeca where the conversational topics ranged freely from Wittgenstein to three-picture deals and back to Wittgenstein. On a recent visit the owner had called Harry's integrity into question— which made it difficult for him to go back. Until the insult, Harry had had a fine time at that bar throughout the years. But he also enjoyed himself at Nunzi's. Who said that one had to cancel out the other?

"What you have going here," he had once told Nunzi, "is a salon."

And Nunzi had loved hearing that. But Harry had also once suggested that Nunzi organized the groups just for him. It was presumptuous of him to think that, but he had just come off a big picture and was feeling his oats.

"Yeah," said Nunzi dismissively when Harry brought this up. "Like I'm really doing this for your benefit."

And then one day Harry came straight over from the railroad station in Jamaica without calling in advance. Not to check up or anything—he would never do that—but it seemed like too much trouble to put down his bag and fish out a quarter and call. He had called up from the lobby. And sure enough, there were twin hookers from Tennessee in the apartment, along with the son of a former studio head. The girls were staying with Nunzi, who had known their mother, until they got a toehold in Manhattan. They took Harry into the bedroom and showed him their hometown scrapbook. It was filled with pictures of members of the different high-school teams and also the obituary of a boy they knew who had been killed in an auto accident.

So Nunzi really did have a salon, and it had nothing to do with Harry.

The doorman called up and said there was a man there to pick up some money. Nunzi said to send him right up. The fellow was middle-aged and wore a flowered shirt and open-toed sandals. The minute he walked in, Nunzi began to berate him. It seemed he had directed a porno flick that was sponsored by Nunzi, who felt he had shot too many extreme close-ups.

"There's no overall," said Nunzi, who hadn't bothered to introduce the man. "You can't tell what the fuck is going on."

"I've made it clear to you," said the man with a show of dignity, "that my specialty is erotica."

"Bullshit," said Nunzi. "I didn't pay for no medical journal."

"You should see what he does," said Nunzi, appealing to Harry. "He puts the camera right up the girls' cracks."

"It probably made them uncomfortable," said Harry.

"It made *everybody* uncomfortable," said Nunzi. "Would you like to see what this asshole shot?"

Harry said he preferred not to. Maybe sometime, but not just then. Marge's friend said she hoped to start a country-and-western band someday, but no one picked up on that.

The man in the flowered shirt slid to the floor at Harry's feet.

"It all began with my need to look up girls' bloomers," he said, as if he were beginning his life story. "That's what we called panties then."

"Hey, hey," said Nunzi, running over suspiciously. "Anything you two do is with me."

The man looked at Nunzi scornfully and pulled some floodlights out of a closet. When he had set them up, he took a video camera out of his bag and began to photograph the group. Marge's friend threw up a hand as if to ward off a blow, but the former child star woke up and quickly put on his pants.

"Quiet on the set," he said as he joined the group.

Far from objecting to the activity, Nunzi grabbed a fistful of his crotch and went from one person to another, saying: "Please speak into the microphone."

He was supposed to have a big cock, but Harry noticed that he was only working with his balls. When the director began to move in for his fabled close-ups, Nunzi lost his patience.

"Let me have that," he said, grabbing the camera. "Or maybe you're worried that you weren't up everybody's crack enough."

"Jesus Christ, get off my back for a change," said the man, slinking away as if he had been whipped.

"I can direct this," said Nunzi, panning around the room. "I should have directed the other one."

The girl came in from the other room and said, "This means I'll have to straighten out his books. They're such a mess."

She began to shuffle through some papers in a skinny file, and then stopped to read one in particular.

"This is a fucking paternity suit," she said in outrage.

"I told you about that," said Nunzi, holding the camera at what he felt was the proper distance from the group.

"Ennunzio Capabianco," she said with a flounce and a small-town stamp of her foot, "you did no such thing."

"It's over," he said. "I paid the guy twenty-two hundred to write a letter."

"He had to go to school for that," said the girl.

"I give him blow, don't I?" said Nunzi, thereby sealing off the argument.

Harry was not overly concerned about being photographed. His signed poster was on the wall, so he figured he might as well go the distance. But Harry decided he liked Nunzi least as an auteur.

Marge and her friend prepared to leave. So did the man in the flowered shirt; he gathered up his equipment and said he thought one of Harry's pictures was brilliant.

"I felt it stunk when I saw it the first time, but a personal setback caused me to reconsider."

Harry said he liked it when he had handed it in, but the producer's nephew had tinkered with it and he didn't care for the result.

"They're something out there, aren't they?" said the man.

Marge's friend asked Harry if he thought she would be effective as the host of a cable TV interview show.

"If so, perhaps you have a contact."

Harry said that as a matter of fact she probably would be good in such a role, but he didn't have that particular kind of contact.

"Fucked again," she said, her shoulders sagging.

"Maybe that will stop," he said consolingly.

When Marge and her friend and the man in the flowered shirt had left, Nunzi asked why Harry hadn't gone after the friend.

"She wanted to suck your dick," said Nunzi.

"I didn't know that," said Harry, who had never left the apartment with any of the women he ran into at Nunzi's place. Not that it was an iron-clad rule. But it wasn't why he was there.

Nunzi asked Harry if he should pay the man in the flowered shirt.

"I can tell him it's not only me, it's the 'noses' who don't like pictures up a girl's crack. It's my money, but he doesn't have to know that."

When Nunzi said "noses," he put a finger on his own nose and pushed it to the side, which Harry did not feel was necessary. He got the idea.

Harry said it probably wasn't intelligent to have the man running around town saying he had been stiffed.

"You're right," said Nunzi, "but he's not getting a nickel in overtime."

The girl got down on her knees in a prayer position.

"Can we *please* go out?" she asked.

"What do you think, Harry?" asked Nunzi.

"Why not," said Harry.

He had not spent much time bouncing around with Nunzi, but he had enjoyed himself the few times he had. Nunzi was always receiving invitations to the openings of new restaurants that were going to be "the next Elio's" or "the next Elaine's." Just as soon as they got the fixtures in. He was on a great list.

"I'll fetch the car," said the old man.

When Nunzi and the girl went into the bedroom to get dressed, Harry finished up the coke that was on the table. All he had to do was use up what was in his wallet and he would be on his way to achieving his goal, which was to not have any. He still liked it, but he could no longer handle the back end. A logical question would have been why bother with it in the first place? The answer is that Harry didn't, except when he was in the city. So if he was a junkie—and he was not about to argue the point—he certainly was an odd variety. For example, if you put a pound of it in front of him in the country, he would continue on about his business. The same went for Los Angeles. He had been taken to a club in the downtown area where it was listed on the menu and you could order it up like a shrimp cocktail. Harry could not get over that. Yet he had never gone back. It was only when he crossed the bridge to Manhattan that he had to have some. Getting out of the city without a taste would have been brutal. He had asked Matty about this, which may have been a mistake since he was a major player in the industry. But Matty had once categorized Harry as a dabbler, which he liked hearing. And he had a way of getting to the heart of things. Matty said it was simple—associations. But which ones? The bars in which he first discovered dope were either boarded up or had been converted to Tex-Mex restaurants. The women he took it with were in California making more money than Harry. He had sat across the table from one who had rejected his pitches. Other acquaintances from that time were in jail.

So that left Nunzi as an explanation.

The woman who had first taken him to Nunzi's apartment had said: "You will love this man. He's the best of the second rate."

But Harry was beginning to think he was better than that. And besides, who was she, with her bullshit costume jewelry, to talk second rate? And who was Harry to go along with it? If you took

Nunzi out of the picture, would Harry try to replace him? With another Nunzi? He didn't think so. So he may have underestimated the skinny little fuck.

By the time the old man brought the car around to the front of the building, it had started to rain. In line with his classiness motif, he had exchanged his beret for a peaked chauffeur's cap. Harry could not imagine what kind of driver the old man would be and was pleased to see that he was a gentle one. Only once did he make a sudden move into another lane when none was required.

"Wheel man," said Nunzi, by way of explanation.

Harry didn't bother to look at the signs, but he sensed they were headed farther out in Queens. He could not make up his mind about the girl's perfume.

"It's heavy," she said, as if sensing his uncertainty, "but I can't help it. I use it, anyway."

She squirmed about in her seat a lot, and although he couldn't recall for sure, there may have been something about her being pregnant.

The old man pulled up alongside a cemetery.

"I'm glad we went out," said the girl, "and that I wore my best dress."

"Do you want me to take care of business or what?" said Nunzi.

The girl crossed her arms and fumed as if she had been stood up by a date, which in a sense is what had happened. She did a lot of fuming.

Harry followed Nunzi and the old man to a section of the cemetery that seemed to be reserved for people of Oriental descent. A Chinese man was on his knees weeping at one of the graves. He had bloodshot eyes and smelled of whiskey.

"Hey, buddy," said Nunzi, tapping him on the shoulder, "would you mind? We got work to do."

The man looked uncomprehendingly at Harry, who nodded in Nunzi's direction.

"All right, stay there," said Nunzi.

He cleared some refuse from the gravestone of a World War II hero and put it in a waste-disposal bin. Then he and the old man fluffed up some of the neighboring flower arrangements.

"You're right," he said as Harry's ethical guidance took hold. "Guy's got his wife under there and I'm telling him to move his ass."

"I'd like to get married," said the old man, stopping to look up at the sky. "I got a twenty-two-year-old in Bay Shore who really knows how to fuck. She's clean too."

"She's clean?" said Nunzi. "I didn't know that. Then you better go get married."

Nunzi and the old man bent to straighten up a tilted tombstone. Harry moved in to help, but the dope had sapped his strength and he wasn't particularly useful.

"Hey, Nunz," said the old man, "remember the kid they threw in the block who had a pussy *and* a dick?"

This appeared to be a reference to a treat they had shared in prison.

"Yeah, yeah," said Nunzi, recalling the episode. "We ate him right up."

When the stone was erect, they all dusted off their hands. The Chinese man, still on his knees, asked Harry if everything was all right.

"Fine," said Harry.

"Family?" he asked. It was as if he were running a restaurant.

"They're good too."

He got to his feet and offered Harry a bottle of rum.

"Send over a drink," he said with an eager nod.

Harry declined, and so did the others.

"Say hello to the family," said the man as they moved off.

"Fucking guy's pissed," said Nunzi.

"Maybe when he's out here," said Harry.

The girl was still irritable when they got back to the car.

59

"Where to now?" she said. "The lumberyard?"

"I'm getting eighty a week," said Nunzi. "You want me to give that up?"

"I can make five hundred in one afternoon," she said.

"What do you mean by that?" said Nunzi warily.

"You can take it any way you like," she said, crossing her arms like a prom queen.

The girl squirmed around some more and they started back to the city. Nunzi asked Harry if he should ask for more than eighty, and Harry said no, the figure sounded about right.

"All those crosses out there," said the girl with a shiver. "I'm sure glad I'm not dead."

Harry thought of his own folks, who were buried in the Jersey flats. He had never visited the graves and wasn't sure he could find them. When Megan asked about Harry's mom and dad, Harry said he carried them in his heart.

"They aren't squooshed or anything, are they?" she asked.

He assured her they weren't. But you would think he would be able to get out there once. What was he, ashamed of them or something?

He thought of Ziffren, who might be going into a grave of his own.

"A friend of mine started to faint a lot," he told Nunzi. "I'm worried about him."

"Send him one of those little TV sets," said Nunzi.

It wasn't a bad idea, but Harry knew that if he didn't buy one quickly, he wouldn't do it at all.

〰〰 THEY PULLED UP ALONGSIDE A RESTAU-
rant that specialized in caviar. Harry would match his
love for the delicacy against anyone's. Whenever he
made a score in Hollywood, that was one of the first
things he did, have an ounce of it sent up to his room with
all the trimmings. He liked the trimmings almost as much
as he did the caviar.

The old man left the car double-parked in the rain, right outside
the restaurant. It was like sending up a flare for the police, but that
didn't seem to bother anyone. Nunzi ordered an ounce of caviar
for each person at the table.

It was the second most expensive kind on the menu and was a
little pasty. This was disappointing to Harry, since it meant he
wouldn't get the crisp pop that he liked when he bit into it. But
who was he to complain? They all had ice-cold vodka in tall,
thin-stemmed glasses. It had some pepper in it. The old man drank
his with a pinkie extended.

Nunzi passed around some dope that he had dissolved in a
nose-drop bottle so that you could have some right out in public.
Harry sat beside the girl and enjoyed the freedom of being next
to a pretty woman and not having to come on to her. Sipping the
ice-cold vodka and eating the caviar, watching the reflection of the
overhead crystal as it bounced off each of their glasses, feeling high
and frozen himself, Harry wondered for a moment what on earth
he was doing in the country. Was it to avoid nights like this one?

And then, to top it off, a miracle happened: Harry saw a way
to inject some conflict into his Spanish Armada play. In his concentration on the Duke of Medina Sedonia, he had forgotten all about

61

Drake. And that the great sea dog, along with his impoverished family, had had to hang his laundry out to dry on the bowsprit of a beached merchant ship. Surely he must have carried the shame of that experience with him throughout his days. If that didn't produce a little conflict in Harry's play, he didn't know what would. Harry wasn't quite sure how to use the laundry material . . . maybe the memory of it would make Drake try all the harder to defeat the Armada. Or the Duke might needle him about it with a ship-to-ship drumroll. There were all kinds of ways to go. He decided to try out the idea on the group at the table.

Nunzi just shook his head in disbelief.

"Fuckin' guy like that hung his laundry out on a *bowsprit?*" he said. "What was wrong with him?"

"Crude," said the old man.

"It's amazing," said Harry, "how you can work on something for years and then all of a sudden it comes into focus."

"But it *did* come into focus," said Nunzi. "That's what's important."

"Here's to your success, babe," he said, raising his glass in a toast. "Only this time you don't let them fuck you."

Harry was hoping Nunzi would follow up the toast with another round of caviar, but he didn't. Instead he called for the check. Harry made a note to reciprocate in the very near future. The only adjustment he would make is that he would order the good caviar, although he would be careful not to have it come off as a put-down.

They went to a big, friendly bar at which Harry immediately felt comfortable. It wasn't trying to be the next P.J. Clarke's or the next Pietro's. It was content to be what it was. Harry wasn't ready just yet to go back to the writers' bar at which his integrity had been called into question. He wasn't saying that he would never go back. But he needed to cool off for a while. In the meantime the big, friendly bar would serve as an excellent backup. It catered to noses and people in the entertainment world.

Nunzi laid him in with the man who had thought of this mix. He wore an open-collared sport shirt and had a wide neck and big bony fingers; before opening the bar, he had previously enjoyed great success in the fabric business.

After Nunzi had listed Harry's credits, the man said that Coppola had told him he was an interesting type for the movies.

"Did you hear that?" said Nunzi. "Coppola said he would be an interesting type for the movies."

"I did hear it," said Harry. "And if Coppola said that, there must be something to it."

The man considered that for a while and then said that Harry was free to come into his place anytime. It was nice to have that assurance.

"And if you have something for me," said the man, "I'll take that too."

"Without question."

He wondered where people got the idea that lowly screenwriters could get them a part in a movie.

Harry looked around and didn't see any noses or people in the entertainment world, although there may have been some people there who *were* noses but didn't look as if they were. The same with people in the entertainment world. He did spot a journalist he knew whose hard-hitting investigative reporting had toppled a legislature. He dated anchorwomen now and was in the bars a lot and there were indications that he had toppled his last legislature. Still, as Harry pointed out to a detractor, how many of us even get to topple one? Harry liked this man and enjoyed getting his take, for example, on such issues as Japan's unwillingness to take its proper place as a major power. He went over to get one of these takes, and Nunzi joined him, bouncing up and down on his toes and looking from one man to the other. He seemed to want to be worked into the conversation, but apart from introducing him, Harry didn't know how to go about doing that. From the back, however, and at a distance, it might have appeared to an observer that he had been worked in.

Harry looked over at the bar and spotted a pretty, dark-haired girl he knew. He was spotting a lot of people he would normally expect to find at the downtown writers' bar. Was it possible that their integrity had been called into question too? After a night of bending over to put money in a jukebox, the girl had rejected Harry on the basis of his being too old for her. This probably did not speak well for her character, but she was a spectacular flirt and he was wondering if he should give her another try, anyway. While he was mulling this over, Nunzi took his arm and steered him to the table of a brash young comic who had been making waves in the clubs. He was a little too brash for Harry's taste, but he was familiar with Harry's two big pictures, which took away some of the brashness.

"How do I get in touch with a guy like you?" asked the comic.

Before Harry could answer, Nunzi broke in and said: "Through me."

The comic shrugged and Harry shrugged back at him. They understood each other.

But Harry was pissed off. It meant that anything he did with the comic had to go through Nunzi. If Warner's called Harry directly and said they wanted to wire up Harry and the comic on a project, he would have to tell Warner's to speak to Nunzi. And he could just about imagine how anxious Warner's would be to do that. Not that Warner's hadn't dealt with worse. Who the fuck was Warner's? And not that Harry's agency was doing such a great job for him.

Additionally, Nunzi had inflated ideas of how much things were worth in Hollywood.

"What should I ask for, Harry," he would say. "Four million?"

Harry felt that Nunzi was way out of line this time. Yes, he had introduced Harry to the comic, but when Harry brought the tennis pro up to see Nunzi and Sven made it a regular stop, did Harry ask for a cut? When he did a critique of the horseshit screenplay about the cosmos and saved Nunzi a fortune by telling him to stay away from it, did Harry send him a bill? No. As much of a pain in the ass as it was, Harry saw it as a gesture of friendship.

THE CURRENT CLIMATE

How come Nunzi was in on his action and he was not in on Nunzi's?

So that settled it. He had to get away. If he didn't move quickly, Nunzi would start in on how the summer was approaching—and that he might be out in Harry's area. What was it like out there? he would ask. And once again Harry would have to tell him that it was fine out there, but that he had this harmony going with Julie and Megan and the house. And how he didn't even invite his own sister out for fear of disrupting that harmony.

Harry looked for a way to make a graceful exit. Then he told himself the hell with the graceful part and simply said it was time for him to get on his horse.

"What's your rush?" said Nunzi as Harry got up to leave. "We're going to check out the modeling agency."

And Harry sat back down again.

There was something about a modeling agency. Except for this one. And Harry should have known better. What kind of a modeling agency stayed open in the middle of the night? It occupied the penthouse of a building that you would not have expected to have one. The space itself wasn't bad. There was lots of it. And there were rattan furnishings and some nice plants in the reception area; if you squinted your eyes, it would have looked like a halfway decent modeling agency. There was a painting on the wall that was supposed to be by Zero Mostel. But the space was all chewed away at the edges. It had half a kitchen and half a dressing room. You wouldn't want to walk too far in any direction. Harry went out to the terrace, which had a spattered view of New Jersey. Then he started to go through something and had to scramble back inside. That could have been it, right there.

The old man passed around iced 7-Ups while Nunzi manned the phone.

Before they left the big, friendly bar, he had given the girl permission to go dancing with a girlfriend.

65

Nunzi told the callers to send in eight-by-ten glossies. He was very kind to them. But what kind of models called at this hour? And what kind of jobs would Nunzi get for them? Nunzi tossed over a pile of résumés that failed to interest Harry. If the models had been there in person, that would have been one thing. But just looking at the résumés was worse than not having anything to do with models.

One finally did show up, a male one. He had a boyishly eager style, as if he had just come in from Kansas and was determined to make it in the big city. On closer inspection, his vitality seemed faded. He looked as if he had been around for a while and was on his last legs.

"So what have you been doing?" Nunzi asked him as he looked at other people's pictures.

He said he had worked for the man in the flowered shirt.

"Oh, yeah," said Nunzi, perking up. "That means he must have had the camera up your ass for the whole time."

As if to dispel this impression, the model broke into a chorus of "Try to Remember" from *The Fantastiks.* His voice was so thin and frail that Harry had to strain to make out the lyrics. He sang as if he were being washed out to sea. Yet it was affecting. Harry thought of referring him to his friend who produced shows in the off-Broadway theater. But Rene was hanging on by his thumbs. If he'd sent over the model, he could hear Rene saying: "That's some favor you did me. Why not send him to the Surgeon General and get it over with."

And then he would probably ask about the Spanish Armada play that Harry had promised to deliver.

"How's it coming along? What's it got, one hundred and forty-two characters? That'll really bail us out."

Rene was convinced that Harry saved all of his reasonable projects for Hollywood. So Harry decided to stay out of it.

After thanking Nunzi for his consideration, the model dropped off his résumé and left. Harry didn't even want to think about his next appointment.

THE CURRENT CLIMATE

The male model cinched it. Harry said he really had to get going. And Nunzi was surprisingly gracious about it. On the other hand, what was he supposed to do, wrestle Harry to the ground to keep him there?

The two men gave each other hugs, Nunzi saying it was always a pleasure to hang out with Harry. The old man said "Ta-ta" and enclosed Harry's hand in his own as if it were a baby sparrow. And Harry was no slimbones.

Harry felt terribly relieved as he made his way out to the corridor. But he could not remember if he had come up on the stairs or used the elevator. That was the type of thing that the dope did. He decided to try the stairs, but after a few steps down, they crumbled away to nowhere. And he may have seen half of something small go scurrying by. So he went back up to the landing and called for the elevator. He got inside and rang the down button and he could tell by the ponderous way in which the doors closed that he had made a mistake.

〰〰 THE ELEVATOR DESCENDED SLOWLY, with Harry cheering it on. And then it stopped. Oh, shit, Harry thought, it has finally happened. His days of getting away with it were over. Other than the up and down buttons, there weren't any others to press. The elevator was some kind of scaled-down industrial model. Harry jumped up and down a little to try to get it started, and when that didn't work, he smacked the walls a few times, but mostly for dramatic effect. It certainly was sturdy; he had to give it that. Apart from letting out a primal scream, that took care of his options. And he wasn't one of those people.

Suffocating was Harry's least favorite thing to have happen. He would rather be hit by a truck any day. But it didn't appear that he was going to have a say in the matter.

And what a shitty time for this. Just when he was about to break through on his Armada play with the new material about Drake's laundry. And when it looked as if there was a revival of interest in his dog show. Now some L.A. sonofabitch would probably round out the concept and cash in on Harry's rottweiler research. He hoped they would at least throw Julie a few dollars.

He felt awful about Megan too. Not the shame of it so much. It wasn't as if people would say: "There's the little girl whose cokehead father got caught in the elevator of a bullshit modeling agency."

What bothered Harry is that she would be turned over to another dad. Julie loved him, but he had always told her that if he dropped out before she did, to go ahead and snap up someone else after a decent period of mourning. She could do it too. Once she

68

set her mind to it, she could charm the ass off anybody. He could think of a couple of people who wouldn't even have to be charmed. They were ready to go.

And who could blame her. But then Harry would have to be buried alone. It was too late to ask that he be dropped in next to his parents. Or even next to his sister, for that matter.

So much for putting things off.

In the time it took him to have these thoughts, Harry thought surely that something would happen to get him out of there. It always had, but it didn't this time.

What he had to worry about was going over the edge. Not that it would have made any difference. He sat down in a corner, as if there were less chance of freaking that way. When he started to go, anyway, he clamped a hand dramatically over his nose and mouth. It was a technique for dealing with bad news that had been taught to him by Ziffren. But he was on his way. He got to his feet and reached out, but there was nothing to grab.

~~~ WHEN HARRY CAME TO, HE WAS HALF IN
and half out of the elevator. The door had been pried
open as if by a giant can opener.

Nunzi stood over him, eating what smelled like vegeta-
ble soup from a paper cup. He rocked back and forth on
his heels as if he were in a synagogue.

"What happened to you, man?" he asked.

"I got stuck in there," said Harry.

"I know that," said Nunzi with irritation. "But you could have
been in there for a month."

"Hey, listen," said Harry, "I'm the one who was in there."

"Yeah, yeah," said Nunzi, chuckling at this oversight on his
part. "Your ass was stuck in there and we're upstairs talking to
broads."

"Exactly," said Harry.

He got up carefully.

"Have a little tootsky," said Nunzi, offering him a conciliatory
taste.

"No thanks," said Harry.

The word alone was enough to get him off dope.

"Then stay here a minute and rest," said Nunzi. "Marvin went
to get oxygen. We bought a crate off a guy."

"I don't really want any," said Harry. "I need some actual air."

"What do you think oxygen is?" said Nunzi. "It's better than
fuckin' air."

"It might be too pure," said Harry.

"Listen to this," said Nunzi, appealing to an invisible person.
"It might be too pure.

THE CURRENT CLIMATE

"How am I supposed to unload it?" he asked Harry.

"You'll think of something. And I'll see you around."

"All right, all right," said Nunzi, scraping to get the last of the soup. "Go. But it's a good thing we tore you out of there. Otherwise you would have been fucked."

Harry walked outside, still wondering why Nunzi had scolded him. It was his elevator that was at fault. When was the last time he had had it inspected, the Depression?

He made a vow to think twice before going to some crappy modeling agency in the middle of the night. At the same time he tried to put a positive face on the experience. For example, he could use his feeling of helplessness in the elevator for the Armada play. It must have been the same way that the Duke of Medina Sedonia felt when Garabelli's hell-ship bore down on him off the Coast of Flanders.

One thing about Harry is that he had great bounce-back. He could be in the toilet one minute and come flying out of the gate the next. Even now, as he approached the avenue, he was no longer worried about passing out. That was behind him. Still, it entered his mind that he'd recently had to deal with a new kind of episode. The elevator, the anonymous letter, a spooky little urologist in the village who slipped and cut off a corner of his dick . . . No longer was Harry able to sit back comfortably and observe life, as if it were a show being put on for his entertainment. He was being yanked onstage as part of the performance. And if there was anything Harry disliked, it was audience participation.

An intelligent move would have been to go back to the hotel and pack it in. Maybe take another shot at *The Age of Innocence*, which he had brought along, then get up early and have a great hotel breakfast. Even though the food was generally lousy, they did a good job on this one meal. Many a morning he had slid out of there with dark glasses and seen businessmen sitting on banquettes, leafing through the *Wall Street Journal* and eating these great stately breakfasts.

71

But it was still early. If he followed that scenario, it would mean crossing off the evening. And he had all that blow left. What he needed to do was regroup. Normally he would do that at the writers' hangout, but the attack on his integrity still rankled, even though it probably had more to do with Charmaine's personal life than with Harry. It wasn't as if he'd pissed in the soup.

He popped into an alley for a couple of quick hits and remembered a theater bar nearby.

Harry immediately became interested in the bartender. She had soft brown hair and a great ass and the kind of subtle good looks that made you feel that you were the only one who had noticed her. Harry began to talk to her as if he didn't know she had a great ass. His mouth was a little stiff from the dope, and he had moved into his Joe Cocker phase, but she listened to him patiently as he struggled to get the words out. She said she was from Arizona and that her father was a psychiatrist. Two surprises and all of a sudden he was screamingly in love with her. So he had to back off quickly. He wasn't allowed to fall in love with anyone. Julie had put her foot down on that. And it would fuck up everything. So he took a deep breath, accepting the pain, and turned to an older woman one stool over.

She wore a black netted dress and youthfully netted stockings and was spectacularly ugly. Harry recognized her as being a *jolie-laide.* He had heard about them and now there was one sitting next to him. Harry struck up a conversation with her, and before he knew it, she was dabbing at her eyes and looking off with a sigh.

"Is there anything wrong?" he asked.

"No, no," she said. "It's just that you are terribly dangerous. But of course that's always been your charm, *n'est-ce pas?*"

Now what on earth could Harry say to that? And how could he not like hearing it? He certainly was starting to get interested in her. She smelled like dying lilacs and lived in a town house in Paris on the Rue de Bac. She said she was confident that friends of hers would be familiar with his work. But only certain ones. The bartender kept serving them drinks and didn't seem the least bit annoyed about Harry's interest in the woman, which was further testimony of how terrific the bartender was.

Increasingly, the *jolie-laide* began to look like Charles de Gaulle. But it didn't stop Harry. The great thing was that he would be able to tell Julie all about her. In fact, he could hardly *wait* to tell Julie about her so that he could get points for being fascinated by a homely woman. There was no reason to tell her about the bartender.

So in the space of twenty minutes Harry had two situations going. Julie, the blarney-face, had always complimented him on his ability to get things going in strange places, although the job of reining him in usually fell to her. He chuckled to himself about this and wished she was there so he could give her a good hug.

A familiar-looking man in a white starched shirt with the sleeves rolled up kept looking over at Harry. It turned out to be Ron. The reason Harry hadn't recognized him immediately was that Ron had darkened up his hair a bit and slicked it over to one side. It changed his look completely, pushing him over into the Bill Hurt area. Hurt was an actor that Harry could watch in just about anything.

Harry excused himself to the *jolie-laide.*

"Why not?" she said with a shrug. "I am used to that."

He could see that the romantically whipped style, plus the extreme homeliness, would get her points in some circles—so long as she held on to the town house.

Harry joined Ron, who explained his presence in the city: He supplemented his income as a hair colorist by spending several nights a week bartendering. Harry was not overly fond of that word. But he noticed that Ron seemed more dimensional in the city. He didn't just whip back and forth from Comedy to Tragedy. And Harry certainly liked Ron's city look. By rolling up the sleeves of a simple white starched shirt and needing a shave, he had created a stark and dramatic effect.

They both agreed it was too bad about Ziffren's fainting spells.

73

"It was his wife's idea for him to get his hair colored," said Ron.

"It just shows you," said Harry. "I thought it was his."

"Oh, no," said Ron. "He would never have gotten it colored on his own."

Harry considered that for a moment. And then Ron, showing that other dimension, slid into his idea for a movie. Normally Harry headed for the door when people did that, but he stayed put on this occasion. There wasn't much more to Ron's notion than a young man following his father to a train station in a small town and then running after the train when it left with his father on it. There may have been some silo material in there too. It didn't sound like much, but Ron's delivery was so vivid that Harry was able to see that father and see that train. Obviously it would have to be fleshed out, but Harry thought about pitching it to a friend at Universal; he didn't mention this to Ron, since there was no point in getting his hopes up.

The story had created an intimacy between them which both men drew back from, Ron stretching out his arms and saying that there did not seem to be much pussy around. Harry said that he could say that again.

As if in response, the *jolie-laide* approached them.

"Fuck you, buddies," she said, and then made her way unsteadily to the door.

"Jesus," said Ron when she left, "what a kisser."

Harry said she was oddly appealing when you got to know her. But actually, he felt she had blown the whole *jolie-laide* persona with her exit line.

Ron said he knew of a place where there might be some action, and Harry told him to lead the way. The bartender was bent over the books near the cash register. She still had the great ass, but Harry decided on a clean break and simply waved good-bye to her. Maybe he would pop in there again.

On the street corner outside, traffic lights came at them from every direction. Harry asked Ron if he would like a little blow.

THE CURRENT CLIMATE

With just the slightest trace of sanctimony, Ron said he rarely used it but then took quite a healthy snort of it for himself.

They each put an arm over the other's shoulder and set off down the street, Harry congratulating himself on having a great new friend. And a surprisingly sensitive one, too, as evidenced by the poignant train-station concept.

There were only a handful of women at the club Ron took them to. They were with dank and gloomy men who were dressed unseasonably in three-quarter-length leather jackets. All of these outfits seemed to have been purchased at the same store. In sudden bursts of ribaldry, one man would pound another across the chest with the back of his hand. Then the men became dank and gloomy again.

A black man danced flamboyantly with a woman in the middle of the small dance floor. The men looked on disapprovingly but let it go on all the same. Harry figured they were young noses.

Harry and Ron asked two of the girls to dance. They accepted and did a few tentative steps before excusing themselves and drifting back to the circle of men. So Harry and Ron continued dancing together. It seemed like the most natural thing in the world; so much so that he could hardly wait to tell Julie about it. He would say he had spent the night dancing away with a hair colorist.

"You didn't," she'd say.

"The hell I didn't," he'd answer.

"Oh, my God," she would say with fake resignation. "Now I've got to worry about *that.*"

Had he ever lucked out with Julie. He could tell her just about anything.

Harry ran out of gas and left Ron to finish up the dance with the black man and his partner. He joined the two women and their friends in the shadows and said it certainly was a slow night, wasn't it.

"Go somewhere else," said one of the gloomy men.

Harry felt as if he'd gotten one of those sudden blows across the chest. He said that wasn't a bad idea and backed away in a move that was less nonchalant than he intended it to be. He collected up Ron and the two of them went outside for another pop on the street corner. Ron said that sometimes he felt he was a little bisexual, and what did Harry think about that? Harry, who had seen this coming a mile away, responded neutrally, saying he had nothing against it.

They let this hang for a while and then Ron backed off a bit.

"I sure could use a woman," he said. "A big, juicy one with a fat ass that I could really get off on."

Harry said he certainly saw what Ron meant. He kept seeing what Ron meant.

"Oh, hell," said Ron. "Let's go back to your hotel room."

And there it was, flushed right out in the open. Harry said he had a driver picking him up in a few hours to take him back to the country.

"Couldn't he wait?" asked Ron.

Harry said he couldn't, and that he might even show up early. But he had had a great time with Ron and would be sure to call him next time he was in the city.

"And I'm still thinking about getting my hair colored too," he said.

"You won't call me," said Ron, turning to face the traffic. "And you won't have your hair colored, either."

"The hell I won't," said Harry.

But Ron was probably right on both counts. Harry felt terribly sorry for Ron. He gave him a hug and kissed him on his wonderful new hair. And then he left him standing in the rain. Ron tried to give the impression he was waiting for a cab, but Harry felt certain that he wasn't going to take one.

Harry walked over to the next avenue, thinking it would have been an inappropriate time for him to make his debut as a gay guy. Maybe if Ron hadn't rushed him . . . Harry had done that enough times to girls and now knew how they felt. And Ron had seemed a little clammy during the hug, although that may have been a result of the dancing.

Still, it was the closest he had come since the angular tennis pro who thrust out his arm at mid-court and said he was starved for love. In that case it had been the way Sven said *love* that tore it. *Lawv* is the way it came out. Harry certainly was finicky.

When he was a safe distance away from Ron, Harry hailed a cab of his own and told the driver to take him uptown to the hotel. He took another pop of the dope, aware that it was brazen of him to do it right out in the open. The driver brought up official discussion topics and then warned Harry not to get him started on them. Don't get him started on Art. Don't get him started on Religion. Harry did not get him started on any of the topics although he sensed that the man was secretly looking for someone to get him started. Harry was anxious to get to his room so that he could spread out on the bed and watch the tapes. On the other hand, the tapes were not going anywhere. And for the type of evening it was turning out to be, it wasn't all that late.

"How would it affect the course of Western Civilization," he asked the driver, "if I were to turn around and see some girls?

"I know, I know," he added. "Don't get you started on Western Civilization."

"I wouldn't mind that," said the driver. "Don't get me started on girls."

Harry was fifty-eight years old, not fifty-seven. He had been seeing Ziffren for twenty-seven years, not twenty.

He lived close to the water, not on it.

He had the sole credit on one big picture, not two.

And he was on his way to see hookers, not girls.

When was Harry going to stop waffling? After all, he was not being interviewed by the Cable News Network. This was for his own private consumption. Who was going to blow the whistle on him?

Yes, they laughed at his jokes; and yes, they sucked his dick;

and yes, he had told them his credits and they had forgotten about the clock one night. But there was a clock and they were hookers, and Harry was a paying customer. A john, if you prefer.

They were girls, too, but that was a separate argument.

He had met them at the bar of a rib joint and bought them a pitcher of margaritas, and they had wound up rolling around together in their motel room. But it was too easy and Harry was not that good. And he was right. He followed them around from one location to another—he was something of a fan—and freaked when he lost track of them and then found them again by accident. They were in Brooklyn and had added on a switchboard and a reception room, filling out the operation with girlfriends from their hometown.

The one he had gotten to like was a bouncy ex-nurse named Nicky. She would start Harry off with a sensual dance that was actually too sincere for his taste. He watched it for her benefit, not his. Then she would stand over him and come down close on shaky, amateurish legs and then go back up again. If you needed a stranger in your life now and then—which appeared to be the case with Harry—this seemed, in the current climate, to be one way to go. Unless, of course, Harry were to go up after her. While he was waiting for her to descend, he could also take a peek at a porno flick, although that tended to confuse him and he would wind up nowhere.

Since Nicky drifted in and out of the business, there was never any certainty that she would be there. So Harry was absolutely thrilled when she greeted him at the door, bouncier than ever in a kimono with a dragon on it. This surprised Harry, since he expected hookers to deteriorate quickly. There was one other person in the reception area, a stocky man who wore sneakers and a brown sweat suit. It bothered Harry that he would have equal access to the girls, but that was part of the package.

Harry followed Nicky into a large room that was decorated in the style of a hunting lodge. He noticed that the sheets were of the same pattern he had at home and tried to block that out.

THE CURRENT CLIMATE

"I have gotten into penis torture," said Nicky, "and I've had to raise my rates."

"I'm not interested in any," said Harry, "but I'll pay you the extra money anyway." After he did, she said she would be right back and left. Harry undressed and arranged his dope on a night table so that he could get at it easily. Then he folded his arms across his chest and looked at the ceiling as if he were in a church. He remained in that position for a while and then felt that too much time had gone by. This set off a faint alarm in his head. But it seemed like an awful lot of trouble to get up and see what was going on, so he stayed put. This turned out to be a mistake. A short, chicken-chested man with a mustache tiptoed in, shut the door behind him, and showed Harry a snub-nosed .45, as if he were offering it for sale. Then he stuck the barrel inside his shirt.

"This is a police raid," said the man. "And it is not your lucky day."

He sounded very sad about this and told Harry to turn over and put his face in the pillow. Try as he might, Harry could not bring himself to do that. There was something about it being a hooker's pillow. Not to speak of what would be happening behind him. Whatever it was, Harry wanted to be in on it.

The fellow tapped Harry sharply behind the ear with the gun and told him to try it again. Harry did his best. But despite his situation, he could not resist taking a peek back through his armpit. The man was going through his billfold. He nodded approvingly at certain items and rejected others. As dreadful as Harry felt, he took comfort in the fact that, after all, the man was a police officer. The worst that could happen is that Harry's name would be listed in the tabloids if they were still doing that. Or maybe it was in New Jersey that they followed that procedure. But then Harry began to wonder about the man. Not so much about his size, since Harry was aware that they had dropped that requirement dramatically. But why would a police officer need to keep him pinned to the bed with a gun while he went through Harry's wallet? Then he realized that the man was not a police officer, after all. Why it took him so long to come to that

79

conclusion was beyond him. He was going to have to stop believing everything people told him.

A second person came into the room. Harry took another one of his peeks and saw that it was the man in the sweat suit. He stuck a gun in Harry's ass. As Harry swatted back at it, the smaller man said: "Hey! Let's have none of that."

"Can't I just work it around a little?"

"I said *knock it off,*" said the first man, who was clearly in charge. The man in the sweat suit did what he was told and left. But Harry could tell by his shuffling gait that he was dissatisfied. And the gun had gotten in there.

"Now Harry," said the man in charge, "you are going to have to keep your head in that pillow."

He had evidently gotten Harry's name from the wallet. Harry tried as hard as he could to comply, but the best he could do was to keep his face an inch away.

He felt that if he did not get a heart attack on this occasion, he would go right through without getting one. He would get other things but not that. Some friends of Harry's who had been through them had described what they were like . . . so Harry knew what to look out for. He wondered if he should share his fear of getting one with the man and decided against it. Instead he waited for a pain unlike any other to fan out across his chest, but the wait was in vain. He was grateful to his Rumanian forebears who must have been a hardy lot.

"Here, Harry," said the man, sticking a plastic card behind his ear.

Harry could not tell which one it was, but he thanked the man, anyway.

"Now Harry," said the man, who seemed to take pleasure in using his name, "the girls are all gathered together in a room downstairs. I would like you to wait five minutes before leaving."

"Hey," said Harry agreeably, "I'm with you. If you say five, it's five. If you want ten, I'll wait ten."

"Five is plenty," said the man.

THE CURRENT CLIMATE

He left then, in almost total silence, so it was hard for Harry to know when to begin his count. To be on the safe side, he threw in some extra minutes. Then he looked up and saw that the man was gone.

He had never been in a room that was that quiet. Nor did he recall ever feeling so naked.

The man had left him his laminated Academy Award membership card. But he had taken just about everything else, including Harry's pants and Jockey shorts. It went without saying that he had taken the dope, too, which really hurt.

Harry waited as long as anyone, in fairness, could have expected him to, and then twirled the sheet around his waist, tying it on one side with a big knot, like a sarong. Then he started down the stairs, expecting at any second to get shot behind his bad ear.

A more humanistic individual would probably have looked in to see if the girls were all right, but Harry just wanted to get out of there. He had the feeling that he would not be seeing this particular group again. And he certainly was not going to ask for his money back.

When he got to the street, his ass began to throb. He had been hoping that it wouldn't, but it did. He thought of stopping in at the Korean market to ask for help. But he had been in there once before to buy a quart of milk—and even that modest purchase had aroused their suspicions. So he could imagine how they would behave if he walked in with no money and a sarong. He got pissed off at the Koreans. Perhaps it was unfair to a great nation—to base his feelings on an experience with a couple of fruit people—but that's the way he felt.

Showing up at an emergency ward was out of the question. He would have to be in much better shape before he did that. There was the hotel, of course. They would probably take him in, sarong and all, and pay the driver. But it would bring the curtain down on the evening in an unsatisfactory way.

So that left the writers' bar where Harry's integrity had been called into question.

81

He had planned to wait six months or so before going back to see if Charmaine would do it again. But this was no time to stand on ceremony. He felt that she would take him in if there was an emergency. He had known her for many years, starting in L.A., where she had been one of the first flower children. A bad marriage to an agent had toughened her up and she had come back East to open the bar, which had immediately attracted writers. The face and the tits didn't hurt.

She and Harry had become good friends. So he had to conclude that there was something going on in her life. And who knows, maybe after twenty years of friendship you were allowed one vicious attack on someone's integrity.

As he drove back to lower Manhattan, he realized that he probably wasn't angry enough at the chicken-chested man with the mustache. He was angry at the Tub of Shit, as the man in the sweat suit would henceforth be known to Harry, but not at the man in charge. Harry was more curious about him. Had he always been a stickup artist or had he switched off from another profession? Did he specialize in whorehouses, knowing it was unlikely that anyone would complain? Where was he now? Had he jumped into a car and sped off to another state? Harry would have enjoyed sitting down with him and asking him these questions. He would even have been willing to guarantee him that he need have no fear of retaliation.

〰〰 WHEN HARRY CAME IN WITH THE SA-
rong, he could tell in one quick glance that it was going
to be all right with Charmaine. Her lips weren't stitched
together the way they were when she had gone after him.

She was seated at a table up front with some young
writers and an ex-detective named Brandywine who had
been forcibly retired from the police department. Charmaine
seemed to be lacing the restaurant with young writers as older ones
like Harry moved away. Harry could tell that the young writers
were hoping to get some ideas from the detective for their sitcoms,
not realizing he would divulge the good stuff only if he was paid
for it. Harry had been around the horn with him. He would tease
them and send them off with an informed feeling, but he would not
tell them shit. Unless he was paid as a technical adviser.

The writer who sat closest to Charmaine was an emaciated lime
with pockmarks. And suddenly Harry knew what the insult was all
about.

"The only reason you are not a scab, Harry," she had said to
him, "is because of your fat bankroll."

As with any insult that hurt, there was some truth to it. Harry
had a six-week cushion and a Spanish Armada play in the works.
How many writers could make that statement? Charmaine's friend
had probably done some light scabbing; she was touchy about it.
Who knows, maybe if Harry had been an emaciated lime with
pockmarks, he would have done some too. Why should the lime
give a shit about an American guild? Harry was alarmed sometimes at how patriotic he could get.

"What the fuck happened?" asked Charmaine.

He saw her pass a hand over the lime's joint. She had done it to Harry once, but the timing had been wrong.

"I got stuck up."

"Now Harry," said Brandywine, playing to the young sitcom writers. "If I told you once, I told you a hundred times to stay away from them cathouses."

Harry winced when he heard this, although no one had ever said Brandywine wasn't intuitive. A little crooked, maybe. The sitcom writers showed some class by not laughing at the remark. They were a good group. And they were probably aware of his credits.

"It took place outside my hotel," said Harry.

"Give him fifty," said Charmaine, signaling to the cashier.

The advance would be put on his tab, but it was the kind of gesture that explained why the restaurant had taken hold.

After Harry had paid the cabdriver, he came back to the restaurant and caught one of the new waitresses looking at him sympathetically. Charmaine had begun to phase out the old Greeks, putting in female replacements and thereby demonstrating her new solidarity with women. The waitress had an appealing gap between her teeth, and a tight body. She also had a neatly sliced panty line showing through her skirt. How do you like that, Harry said to himself. After all that's happened to me tonight, I am still noticing panty lines.

Harry followed her into the kitchen, which was cleaner than he expected it to be. It was the first time he had been back there in twenty years. Maybe that's another reason Charmaine had gotten annoyed with him—that he hadn't taken enough of an interest in her kitchen and how clean it was.

The waitress showed him some slacks that were hanging on hooks in the dessert area. Had other customers come in late at night after having had a gun stuck up their ass? Harry chose a cream-colored pair that he liked a lot. They were full and pleated but fit nicely around the waist. He liked the pants, frankly, more than any of the ones he owned. And he found a linen shirt that wasn't bad either. In the old days he would have told Charmaine to put the pants and the shirt on the tab and kept them; it would have become an official story, to be told by Charmaine to new writers.

When he returned to the table, Charmaine was busy supporting his version of what had happened.

"That's where they work," she explained to the group. "Close to your hotel in an expensive neighborhood."

Her acceptance of his story gave Harry a giddy feeling. Maybe Ziffren was right about lying. There was no telling how far it could get you.

"There were three of them," said Harry, although no one had asked him.

"One," he added, demonstrating, "put a gun right against my temple."

With a backward flip of his palm, Brandywine swept Harry's gun hand aside, at the same time positioning himself so that he was ready to throw a punch.

"Why didn't you do that?" asked Brandywine.

"Yeah, great," said Harry disparagingly, while conceding to himself that it was some move. All night long he had been collecting moves.

Harry ordered a plate of crab cakes and some room-temperature pasta—primarily to get a tab going. Charmaine had added both items to the menu as a means of keeping pace with some new spots in the area that had been influenced by Los Angeles.

"Hey," said one of the sitcom writers, pulling his chair in close to Harry. "If I saw you on the street, I wouldn't fuck with you."

"I wouldn't either," said Harry with some self-importance. "But they did."

"I'm sorry for making light of your situation," said Brandywine, picking up the mood of the table. "It must have been traumatic."

Late one night, in a Squad, he had told Harry the circumstances that had led to his forced departure from the department. It had to do with Brandywine and three men going into a construction site at night and only Brandywine coming out. It's possible he remembered that he had confided in Harry and was being careful with him.

"You call the cops?" asked Charmaine.

"For two hundred dollars?" asked Harry, shaving off one hundred and fifty and leaving out the ass damage.

"Besides," he said portentously, "I'm not finished with it yet."

Charmaine winked at him, buying his bullshit again.

The lime appeared to consider the subject exhausted. Tilting back his chair, he said he loved John Updike so much, he would proudly go down on him. Charmaine led the laughing at this and Harry realized he didn't want to be sitting there with a sore ass, forcing down crab cakes and room-temperature pasta and listening to this conversation. He didn't know anybody there. It wasn't his place anymore.

He pushed his plate aside and signed the check. Then he grabbed the lime by the throat and said that if he caught him scabbing, he would throw him through the front window.

Throwing people through the front window was a tradition at Charmaine's place. She made a show of being upset, but her eyes were hot. She had always liked that side of Harry. And it had been a low-risk move. The lime was a bundle of energy but not much more.

The waitress followed Harry out into the street with his drink, but he said he didn't want it. He kissed her a few times, and although she pushed her pelvis against him, the kisses were tentative. He said something about that.

"Well, do you blame me?" she said.

Again the fucking climate.

"That village you live in," she said. "I was raised there."

He told her to give him a ring if she decided to go back for a visit.

"Thanks," she said. "And by the way, I'm opening my own place down the street.

"Come in sometime. I think you'll like it."

THE CURRENT CLIMATE

* * *

So that took care of Charmaine's. Maybe he would go back there, maybe he wouldn't. Whatever the case, it was going to be different from then on. It was time to move on, although he didn't quite know where. Maybe he should start to take L.A. seriously. He had started to meet a whole new group of authentically witty people out there. Asked to explain this phenomenon, a gay friend of Harry's had said it was because the New York theater had shut down. So all the authentically witty people were now in L.A. It wasn't Harry's imagination.

But this was ridiculous. He was standing in the middle of a tremendous city, teeming with places to hang out. Surely there was one with Harry's name on it.

In the meanwhile, what he really wanted was some dope.

Harry had once heard Nunzi deliver a generalized lecture on the subject of waking him up in the middle of the night for dope.

"What am I, a mutt?" he had said to Harry as he paced the tiny living room in the green robe. "Be a little considerate, don't you agree?"

Harry had said he agreed. So it was with great reluctance that he stopped at a pay phone and called Nunzi in the middle of the night for dope. On top of everything, he asked Nunzi to front him two.

"How much you got?" he asked Harry. "This is business, my friend."

Now Harry was his friend. Harry said he had twenty-six dollars but that he would mail him the rest the next day, which it already was. Nunzi told him to come over. But he didn't seem to love the idea.

As he came up on the elevator, Harry decided to remind him of the Madame de Stael biography—Nunzi thought he was the only one who knew about it—and the time Harry had invested in searching out the rights. Wasn't that business too? Had Harry charged him anything for it?

He was all set to hit Nunzi with this, but it was the girl who opened the door. Her mascara was running in six different directions. She looked like hell, and for the first time Harry did not want to see her body.

"Oh, my God," she said, pointing to the side of his face. "What happened?"

No one at Charmaine's had noticed the condition of his ear. But she had. What he recalled as being a light tap had been something else.

She went into the bathroom and came out with a wet towel, which she applied to the wound. It was Nunzi's towel, but Harry was in pretty deep at this stage, so he let her go ahead.

Nunzi came out of the bedroom looking as if he had aged twenty years since Harry last saw him. Something had gone on back there.

"What the fuck happened to you?" he asked.

Everyone wanted to know what the fuck had happened to Harry.

Harry told him the whole story. He really wrapped himself around the part with the gun in his ass.

"It's a lucky thing he didn't pull the trigger," said Nunzi. "Then you really would have been fucked."

"I know that," said Harry.

"You would have had no ass left."

"Right," said Harry, wondering why Nunzi had to say everything.

"What's the guy look like?" asked Nunzi, turning somber. He stared out of the window as if he could find him out there.

Harry described the chicken-chested man with the mustache.

"We know that guy?" asked Nunzi.

"He doesn't ring a bell," said the old man.

He had been sleeping in a chair with a beret over his face, but he had awakened immediately.

"Let's get him," said Nunzi.

Harry told him to forget it. He hadn't been able to work up any anger toward the man, who had gone about his work in a professional manner. The Tub of Shit was another story. Besides, how were they going to find someone in a city of that size?

THE CURRENT CLIMATE

"What are you worried about?" said Nunzi.

He put on one of the designer-label suits he had purchased earlier that day off a truck. Then he checked himself in a floor-length mirror, smoothing back his hair as he did so. All of a sudden he was presentable. He looked as if he were set to trot right out onstage. The old man stood up and sang "Tea for Two," pronouncing the word *tew* and giving Harry a juicy grin.

On several occasions Harry had seen Nunzi and the old man disappear around a street corner, their heads close together. He had wondered what they were about to do. Whatever it was, he had a feeling he was about to do it with him.

Nunzi walked back into the bedroom to tell the girl they were going out. Harry thought he heard her crying. Then Nunzi came back in and asked Harry why he had paid for pussy.

"You could have come to me," he said.

"I like to get in and get out," said Harry.

"Well, I am tired of seeing you get fucked over," said Nunzi.

In the elevator, Nunzi put his head against Harry's shoulder and started to cry. He said the girl had lost the child. He had gotten someone to come over and paid out two thousand, but it hadn't worked out.

"My fuckin' kid," said Nunzi. "What if it was my last shot?"

Harry said that he would have other shots, but he wasn't that sure about Nunzi as a dad. It raised serious ethical questions.

Nunzi pulled himself together and they went to half a dozen after-hours spots. Harry could not tell them apart. Each one had a man outside in charge of security, but no one had any trouble getting in. There may have been a certain type of individual they were looking for. Each of the spots had a dime-size dance floor and a blackjack table. Harry lingered at one. The odds were such that there was no point in playing—you might as well have handed your money right over to the dealer. But it was something to do. The customers held drinks and stood with their backs to the bar, waiting for something, probably the morning. Only the hookers were animated. They seemed to be glad they were off work. Harry

89

didn't see any point to it all. On the other hand, the places weren't there for him.

He kept insisting to Nunzi and the old man that they shouldn't be doing what they were doing, but he had to admit it was nice to have a little support for a change. It had been a long time since he had been part of a team. But he was fifty-eight now and would probably have to change. Maybe he would look into doubles tennis.

Harry was surprised when they found the two men, although he probably shouldn't have been. On his trips to the city, he had never failed to run across at least one significant person in his life. If you stuck to prescribed pathways, it was a small town.

The chicken-chested man with the mustache sat at the bar with a formal service setting and a complete dinner laid out before him. The Tub of Shit ate a cheeseburger with onion rings.

"That's them," said Harry.

"It is, huh," said Nunzi, hiking up his pants and smoothing back his hair. Harry had never been in on anything like this, so he was uncertain as to how to proceed. And he still felt he was handicapped by his relative lack of anger. He tried to work some up as he approached the pair. Nunzi and the old man fell in behind him, the latter waving to the other customers as if a master of ceremonies had asked him to take a bow.

Feeling it was his responsibility to kick things off, Harry came up behind the smaller man and tapped him lightly on the shoulder.

"What did you do that for?" Harry asked him.

"I am a gangster," the man said, looking up with no particular surprise.

"That's no excuse," said Harry, who noticed that in the time since he had last seen the man, he appeared to have had his hair styled. He had a great set of dentures, too, although Harry had the feeling that they hadn't been in that long.

"Come on, Harry," said the man. "You can take care of yourself. You're a big boy.

"Try the duck," he suggested, turning back to his food.

His nose was like a rain forest; this led to a watery pronunciation of the word *duck* which Harry would never forget. It was probably Harry's dope too.

"I don't want your duck," said Harry, trying to get some heat behind his response but aware that he was vamping. Even with his back-up, he was still afraid of the man. The dope didn't help either. It held him in check, like a cold hand across his neck. It was time for someone else to take over, although Harry did feel he had the man covered for sudden moves.

"How about a zetz?" said the man, turning away from his plate and swiftly producing a vial. "It's good blow."

"You're fucking-A it's good blow," said Nunzi, finally coming in.

"He's with me," said Harry with some pride.

"Then tell him to buy the girls a drink," said the man, gesturing toward three hookers at the end of the bar.

The calm response made Harry even more curious about the man.

"You talkin'," said Nunzi, putting his face up close to the man's. "You talk to me. Talk. What are you talkin'? Talk. Go ahead. Talk. Start talkin'."

It was awful stuff to listen to, but Harry had to assume that Nunzi had done this before and knew how to conduct himself.

Sensing that all was not well, the Tub of Shit looked up from his cheeseburger and said he was the son of a feared nose. And the nephew of one who was even more feared. The old man released his arm in the move that Harry had admired so much and that he had planned to sign up and learn. It cleared out the bottom of the man's face to the extent that Harry was confident he would never again be recognizable. The cheeseburger disappeared way back in there too.

The man with the mustache reached for his ankle, and the old man bent down and snapped it. He was all over the place and frisky as a pup.

"Leeemeee alone," the man said with a groan.

Normally Harry resisted such comparisons, but his voice was

eerily reminiscent of Barbara Stanwyck at her most emotional. Nunzi pulled the .45 out of the man's sock and held it up to the light, as if to appraise it.

"Didn't he go down nice?" said the old man, standing over the Tub of Shit.

"Yeah, yeah," said Nunzi. "Great. Now let's get out of here. I don't want no grief."

Surprisingly little attention was paid to the group as Nunzi and the old man assisted the man with the mustache out the door. He put his arms around them for support. It was as if he had fallen on the street and a pair of Good Samaritans had come to his aid. Nunzi stuck a bill in the pocket of the man at the door, who pulled it out and examined it as if to make sure it was the going rate for this situation. Satisfied, he waved them on.

With Harry bringing up the rear, the procession moved out to the street.

"Hey, Harry," said the man with the mustache. "You're in the movies, right? If you should decide to direct, give me a call."

He certainly was an amazing man. No doubt he had deduced Harry's profession from the Academy Award card. And even though his ankle had been snapped, an outside observer would have guessed that he was the one in charge.

"You talkin', what are you talkin'," said Nunzi, sinking back into that awful patter. "Anything Harry does is with me."

"I would know how to take care of him on the set," said the amazingly calm holdup man.

"You would know bullshit," said Nunzi, who seemed annoyed at being upstaged.

"Where are you taking him?" asked Harry as the old man pulled up the car.

"Leave that to the big boys," said Nunzi.

Harry felt that this was unnecessarily insulting and made a note to bring it up with Nunzi on some future occasion.

As he was being eased into the backseat, the man with the mustache drew back and looked at the car with disdain.

"Why don't you buy a Jag?" he said. "I'll let you have one for fifteen K."

"Yeah, yeah," said Nunzi, shoving him into the car. "Like I need a Jag."

But he seemed to be thinking it over.

As the car drove off, Harry tried not to think of what they were going to do to him. Or what he would owe Nunzi. Unlimited visits to his house? Free screenplays? Access to his wife and daughter? Of course, he hadn't asked for any help. It had been offered to him. It was important to remember that.

As he waited there in the deserted street, Harry thought of bolting for the hotel and losing himself in *The Age of Innocence*. Maybe if he took some notes on the Armada, he would feel better. There was an area involving the Dutch sluices that he hadn't tapped yet. It would be difficult to get the actual sluices onstage, but a reference to them might be useful.

Nunzi and the old man came back around twenty minutes later.

The old man held a hand over his mouth and burped politely as if he had eaten a big meal. Nunzi handed Harry his wallet and his credit cards.

"Thanks," said Harry, "but what did you do? I have to know."

"Hey," said Nunzi, cupping Harry's face with his hands. "Stop worrying your pretty face. I love you, sweetheart. Let somebody do something nice for you once in a while." '

Nunzi kissed Harry on both cheeks, causing the old man to blush. The old man suggested that Harry come sup with him sometime.

Harry couldn't let that go by.

"I don't sup with anybody," he said. "If you want to have dinner, that's fine."

The old man looked confused and started to erupt. But Nunzi stepped in front of him and pulled out some packets.

"All right, let's go," he said, rocking back and forth on his heels. "What do you want, two, three? I don't have all night."

≈≈≈ HARRY WAS SURPRISINGLY CHIPPER when he got back to the hotel. He had the dope and the tapes and there was still some night left over. He took a shower and then powdered himself up as if he were preparing for a date. Then he. put on the terry-cloth shortie bathrobe that had been provided by the hotel and that you were allowed to keep if such was your preference. The only requirement is that the management be informed so that they could add eighty-five dollars to your bill.

Harry told the hotel operator that except for Mrs. Towns he did not want to be disturbed until further notice. That's all he would need is for Twentieth or someone like that to catch him first thing in the morning while he was still a basket case. He had a feeling the operator would give him points for considering his wife and make a special effort to guard his privacy.

Harry then set up the tapes, took a few blasts of the dope, and lay back to enjoy them. After he had watched the new ones, he decided that the automobile-fender sequence in *Better Blondes* was still the one to beat. What was the point of bothering with the others? So he settled in to watch it a few times, but then the phone rang, causing Harry to jump up as if the hotel had been raided. After all his careful instructions, they had let someone through, after all.

Harry felt that this would never have happened at the Carlyle, where he could have stayed for just a few dollars more. But he would have run the risk of encountering industry bigwigs in the elevator while he was coked up.

THE CURRENT CLIMATE

It was the kind of ring that did not show any signs of letting up, so Harry decided he might as well go ahead and pick up. It turned out to be Brandywine, which explained why the call had been allowed through. He would know how to pull that off.

Brandywine hoped he wasn't disturbing Harry.

"No, no, not at all."

"I just want you to know, Harry, that I am on your side in your feud with the cunt."

Harry said he didn't think Charmaine was a cunt. And there was no feud.

"Don't tell me you plan to go back there after the treatment you received."

"I might," said Harry. "Things change. You never know."

"She's a cunt and you know it," said Brandywine.

"I don't think so," said Harry, trying to hold himself together.

"We'll see," said Brandywine.

"So, m'boy," he said, as if settling in for a long session. "How is it up there? I hear they have all the amenities."

"It's just fine," said Harry, wondering why Brandywine was torturing him.

"You wouldn't want me to try to run down those hoodlums, would you. Fucking lowlifes put that shit up their nose and feel they own the city."

"I don't think so," said Harry, wondering if the call could possibly have anything to do with Scrimmage Wounds. The term was used to describe the preliminary, somewhat playful nicks inflicted by slashers before they really got going. Brandywine had told Harry about them at a steakhouse ten years back, and Harry had used the reference in an action-adventure film; he assumed that paying for the expensive dinner evened the account. But Brandywine had brought it up each time they met and seemed to have expected more.

Sure enough, Brandywine told Harry not to worry about the Scrimmage Wounds.

"It was a pleasure to do that for you, and any monetary consideration is out of the question."

Harry said he appreciated that and made a note to send Brandywine a couple of hundred as a settlement.

"Perhaps you'd like some company?" said Brandywine.

"Thanks," said Harry, "but I was just about to pack it."

"In that case," he said significantly, "I'll let you get back to whatever it is you were doing up there."

"Great," said Harry.

Harry tried to pick things up where he had left off, but there was no question that Brandywine had thrown off his rhythm. He had intended to time his ejaculation with the automobile-fender sequence in *Better Blondes.* Instead he lost control during the credits of *Blonde Explosion.* It was a disaster. Lying there in his terry-cloth shortie bathrobe with a dead dick and an automobile-fender sequence on the VCR that he no longer wanted to see, Harry had to concede that the evening had been a bust. And that his dream of having a normal night in the city had come to nothing. Now he would have to drive all the way back to the country with little to show for it.

If it was the last thing he did, however, he was not going to make one of the calls to Julie in which he said he was a washout and when was he going to knock it off. But he did have to talk to someone, and the only one he could come up with was Ziffren. No doubt it was unfeeling of Harry to call a man who may already have dropped dead, but Harry was desperate. A shaft of daylight had slipped through the blinds, ruling out sleep as a possibility. In Harry's world, nighttime was for sleeping and daytime was for being awake. He had never gotten past that. So there was no point in even wasting the vals.

He called Ziffren's office and was switched over to his home. Harry was excited when he heard Ziffren's voice; he could not resist saying to himself: "Thank God."

"It's unusual of you to make a call of this nature," said Ziffren. "What's cooking?"

THE CURRENT CLIMATE

Harry said that something indeed had come up, but first it was important that he hear about Ziffren.

"The tests were a lot of fun," said Ziffren.

"They were?" said Harry, who was immediately curious about them. Not that he wanted to run over and take a few—but how much fun could they have been?

Ziffren suggested that Harry come directly to his home.

"Sounds like you need to see me as a well person."

This implied that Harry had been thinking of nothing but Ziffren's welfare, which was outrageously wide of the mark. Swinishly, he had barely given him a thought. Still, he took the psychiatrist up on his generous offer.

"I'll be out there as soon as possible," said Harry. "Although you never know what you're going to run into on the highway."

"So be it," said Ziffren.

Harry was hardly a new man when he hung up, but he certainly did feel better. The troops were on the way. Still, his ass stubbornly continued to give him trouble, and he could not think of a doctor he felt comfortable about seeing. Harry's dying novelist friend had referred him to one who had treated top society figures in his heyday. Harry had seen him for a sore throat and it had worked out well. He had a great elixir that he gave to people. But presenting his ass to a man who had looked after Mellons and Fords was another story.

In no time flat Harry was packed and on his way. He sailed past the front desk, telling the clerk to bill him directly, and took a quick peek at the restaurant. Sure enough, the executives were seated at their banquettes, enjoying wonderful breakfasts and thumbing through the *WSJ*. Harry wondered if he wanted to be among them. Or was it just the wonderful breakfasts?

Harry took naps along the way, pulling over to the side of the highway and storing up sleep in twenty-minute increments. He had been to the house once before; it was a huge Victorian structure bursting with artifacts that Ziffren had collected on field trips to the Yucatan. Only a small ribbon of property surrounded the house, which annoyed Harry more than it should have. Living in it for Harry would have been like wearing tight shoes. But obviously Ziffren loved it that way.

Harry was greeted at the door by the short but stately Tess Ziffren. She wore a richly brocaded dressing gown and seemed cranky as she led him, in her majestic way, into Ziffren's study. When Ziffren appeared, she cupped her large breasts and said: "My boozies hurt, Stu."

Ziffren seemed fit and well on his way to recovery. He hugged his wife and said, "Well, you got 'em, baby."

"Thank you, darling," she said, and gave him a kiss.

After Tess Ziffren had left, Harry, who wished she hadn't said *boozies,* felt an obligation to tell Ziffren that he had met his colorist in the city.

"Did you discuss me?" said Ziffren sharply.

Harry said they had, but only briefly. Then he described his night in the city.

"You were mugged, eh?" said Ziffren with a chuckle.

"I beg your pardon?" said Harry.

Ziffren said it happened to thousands of people every day.

"They all get a gun stuck up their *toches* in a whorehouse?" said Harry with irritation.

"Exactly," said Ziffren, refusing to be swayed.

Harry wondered why he had switched over to the Yiddishism; possibly it related to a concept he was working on for a Borscht Belt comedian who had gotten hot in film.

"Does that do it?" asked Ziffren.

Harry had never mentioned Nunzi to Ziffren, but he did on this occasion, focusing on the enormous debt he had taken on.

"God knows what he'll ask for," said Harry.

"Forget about him," said Ziffren, shuffling papers as if he were annoyed to have his time taken up with trivia. Amazingly, Harry did.

He handed Harry a little bag of death pamphlets that he had

prepared in advance and said that he would find them useful. Then he said they were going to have to tighten up the visits.

"Let's not forget," he said, "our original contract was for forty-five minutes."

"That's all right with me," said Harry.

As if to prove the point, he jumped to his feet and shot out the door.

But it wasn't all right with Harry. He was pissed off. Surely you would think that after twenty-seven years he would be allowed to go a few minutes over now and then. Still, as he moved out onto the highway, his anger began to fade. No doubt Ziffren had given him a signal to tighten up his life. His ass felt better, too, so maybe it was just the idea of what had happened that had caused the discomfort.

Harry stopped at a roadside stand to get some French fries and ketchup. They were great. He wished he could have thanked the person who thought them up.

When Harry pulled up to the house, Julie's car, mercifully, was not in the driveway. That meant that she had probably taken Megan to either her ballet lesson or her pony lesson or any of the other lessons that were designed to prepare her for everything. And Harry would be able to get a head start on steadying his nerves.

He went into the shed and took a quick pop of the Stolichnaya vodka. Then he gave his Spanish Armada play a quick flip through, knowing it would be two days before he was able to sail into it with full guns. He lay down on the couch for his next nap, but the events of the previous night kept spinning by. In particular, he could not take his mind off the chicken-chested stickup artist and his remarkable composure under pressure. It was with this thought in mind that he decided to call Nunzi.

"Hey, listen," he said, "I want to thank you for helping me out with that guy."

"Anytime, babe," said Nunzi. "You keep forgetting how much I love you. You here?"

Harry said he was in the country.

"How is it out there?" said Nunzi. "It must be beautiful."

"It is," said Harry. "I've never seen anything like it.

"But listen, Nunzi," he added. "About that guy. Anything between you and him is with me."

"What are you talking about?"

"Listen to him," said Harry, to his own invisible bystander. "What am I talking about."

Nunzi was silent for a moment. Then Harry could see his gray smile start to form over the phone.

"You fuckin' guy," said Nunzi.

"No, *you* fuckin' guy," said Harry.

"All right," said Nunzi cheerfully. "When are you coming in? I miss your face already."

"I don't know, Nunz," said Harry. "Right now I have to get my beauty sleep."

And he did too. When he woke up, he didn't know where he was or what time it was. But Julie's car was in the driveway. He calculated that it was early evening, which meant that he had probably been out for five or six hours. Along with the highway naps, he was on his way to his required eight hours of sleep.

He walked back into the house and saw that Julie had thoughtfully laid out a spicy delicatessen spread for him. This was her night to go meet the woman and buy the rest of the horse. They owned half of it, and Harry had told Julie to buy the other half. That was fine, but it meant that he would have to take care of Megan whether he was ready or not.

As he ate his sandwiches and caught up with the newspapers, Harry wondered if he was ever going to have a decent night in the city. Or was he doomed to continue driving in with high hopes, only to veer off at the last second and make a call to Nunzi?

Later he and Megan took a walk down to the lake. They sat in what he thought of as an enchanted glade and speculated on who lived on a scruffy little island nearby. Was it pirates or dwarves or princes? Some swans drifted by. Harry said it was all right to love them but at the same time to remember that they had sharp tempers. That's the reason they lived in the country. So that they could see swans and Harry could tell her about them. But you couldn't keep the world out. She had begun to ask him if everybody had to die and about Chinese people and Eskimos and what it was like for Harry as a boy in the Bronx. He told her he had a friend named Dogmeat and listened to a radio that was built into an artificial fireplace. But she wanted to know more. And that's when Harry saw that there might be a way for him to have a normal time in Manhattan, after all.

"Hey, Megan," he said, lifting her up high to show that she had a strong dad, even if he was a little on the old side. "What would you say to a trip?"

"I'd love it," she said, shrieking out the word *love* and throwing her arms around him.

"Good," he said, setting her down on his lap. "Now let me tell you about a town called New York City."

101

Three

～～ IT WAS AT THE TAIL END OF THE KO-rean War.

As Harry Towns was about to leave the Air Force and drive back East, he was asked if he would mind taking along a short Israeli. He said sure. How could he possibly say no? Harry did not stay up nights worrying about Israel. However, he did think of it as a little bit of a country that was hanging on by its thumbs. A thousand Arabs had been assigned to Harry's base for training in electronics, and the Israelis had only sent over this one short individual. And now they were recalling him. That got Harry nervous. When he met the fellow, he asked him if Israel shouldn't send over a few more people to even things up.

The fellow just shrugged as if to say that one was enough.

Harry welcomed him aboard and told him to leave his gear in the back of the Chevy. If you could call the little bundle he was carrying gear. Harry could just about imagine what was in there. Probably some sad-looking European underwear and maybe an apple. He hoped there weren't a couple of hard-boiled eggs in there too.

They set off for New York City together on a fresh and crisp autumn day. It was Harry's favorite kind of weather. He hadn't even bothered to consult a map. All he knew is that he was out West and if you went out to the highway, hung a left, and kept going, you would be sure to hit the city. And that's the way Harry thought of it too. As the city.

Harry made a few stabs at engaging the Israeli in conversation, asking him if he had enjoyed himself in the Air Force and whether he planned to see any Broadway shows when he got back East. But all he got in response was either a shrug or nothing at all. There were times during the long drive when Harry felt like smacking him around to get something out of him, but obviously he couldn't do that, so he just hummed to fill in the time.

There was no way to get Harry down. He had a pocketful of money the Air Force had given him as a separation bonus. He hadn't even known he was entitled to one, and would have left the Air Force free of charge. But they had insisted on giving it to him. Harry and Sally had agreed that he would go back East and get set up in a job. Then he would send for her and they would get married. Sally had been resigned to the decision if not overjoyed by it; but Mrs. Turner had fixed Harry with a cruel Ukrainian stare that scared the shit out of him. That was after a year of loading him up with veal cutlets and constantly taking him aside to say: "Don't worry, I'm on your side." Harry got along fine with Mr. Turner, who had literally taken a shirt off his back and given it to him when Harry admired it. So who was on the other side? is what Harry wanted to know.

He was happy to get out of there.

Harry paid for the gas and food along the way but at a certain point he would not have minded it if the Israeli had kicked in a few dollars. It's true he had lost his entire family in the camps— Harry forgot who told him that, probably the sergeant—but Harry felt that he should make a small contribution, anyway. Pay for half the gas, anything. Not that Harry needed the money. And not that he would have felt entirely comfortable taking it from a fellow whose whole family had been wiped out in the camps. But it still wasn't right. What was he going to do, get back at the world by being a cheap person? These were probably unconscionable thoughts, but Harry had them, anyway.

After they had checked into a motel, Harry spotted a basketball hoop in the garden, and since neither of them had gotten any exercise, he suggested they play a little one-on-one. Although Harry had a height advantage and was able to pour in jumpers almost at will, the Israeli was surprisingly feisty, especially when it came to lunging after balls that were about to go out of bounds. They both lunged after one such ball at the same time, and when Harry reached it first, the Israeli went for his eyes.

"Holy shit," said Harry when he saw just how serious the Israeli was. He hated to do it, but he was forced to go for the man's jewels in order to get him to loosen his grip. Otherwise that might have been it, with Harry starting out his career as a blindie. It took a long time for them both to calm down.

But they did and soon were seated in the combination restaurant and hunting lodge, enjoying a great dinner that Harry begrudgingly paid for. Then, to make sure they got an early start the next morning, they went straight to bed. Sure enough, the Israeli had the kind of underwear Harry was worried about. It was gray and had flaps on it that had to be unbuttoned if you wanted to go to the john. It looked like the kind that got passed out in deportation centers. But who knows, maybe it was great underwear and it was Harry who was off base. Underwear was such a personal thing. Harry slept uneasily. Great, he thought as he lay there, checking the other bed for movement. Drive a person across the country, pay for his ass, and have to worry about getting your throat cut.

But there was no curbing Harry's elation. He bounded out of bed the next morning, slapped the Israeli on the back, and told him they were going to eat everything on the menu for breakfast and to forget about the money.

At that point the Israeli reached into his bundle and pulled out a few dollar bills. Naturally they were all crumpled up, in case Harry didn't feel bad enough. When Harry saw the condition of the money, he told him to forget about it, it wasn't important. This was his day to see the skyline. And when he did, he almost jumped out of the car.

"Will you look at that sonofabitch, Schmuel?" he said. "Is it something?"

But then he realized that the skyline didn't mean anything to his new friend. He didn't know about Ethel Merman and Ruby

107

Foo's and roasted chestnuts and buying a white gardenia for your mom. When Harry was seeing *Gypsy* at the Winter Garden, Schmuel had been crouched in a corner somewhere, gnawing on a bone. And don't ask what kind of bone it was. If anything, the skyline probably depressed him. So Harry asked him where he wanted to be dropped off. He said he was staying in Ozone Park with a second cousin who was in the insurance business.

"Leave me anywhere," he said.

So Harry thought he might as well let him out right there in Riverdale, and it was only when he saw him standing alone in the street that he fell apart. He wanted to get out of the car and hug him and apologize and bring him home to Glo and put him in a tub and take him to musicals and keep him there as a brother. And just let anybody try to get smart with him. But Harry didn't do that. He was good at thinking of things like that and not following through on them. So he just drove away. He told himself that Schmuel wouldn't have welcomed the offer, anyway. He might have even gone for Harry's eyes again. Or who knows, maybe his second cousin would be better at getting him into musicals than Harry.

Harry did not know exactly what to expect when he got home. Randy had moved up the street and shared an apartment on the boulevard with a woman named Trudy who had straightened out his business affairs and gotten him a position in a brokerage firm. What Randy, who had failed in the shoulder-pad business, was doing in a brokerage firm was beyond Harry. The one time he bought some shares of stock, he stayed up every night for a week worrying about it before he finally sold the shares. But it seemed to be working out. As far as Harry knew, Glo had been coping with this in the best way she could, by going to luncheonettes during the daytime and knocking them back at night. But it had not stopped her from making a quick trip to Joplin when Harry needed help buying the Chevy. Or from riding around with him until he got the hang of driving, which could not have been any fun without a drink. Harry had always felt that if she had stayed in Joplin a few days more, he would not have plowed into the streetcar. But then he would not have met Sally in the wreckage.

In any case, he was happy to see Glo.

Harry parked the Chevy in front of the building and spotted James carrying some venetian blinds into the lobby. He was a big, black, hearty man whom Harry always thought of as being a wonderful person, although he was not sure why. Maybe it was because he was big, black, and hearty. Actually he could get a little cranky on you when his hips hurt.

"Welcome home, Harry," said James. "Glo has gone down the hill for a while and should be back presently. I'm just taking these blinds up to Corman."

He let out a big, booming laugh, which he did after everything he said, whether it was intended to be funny or not.

Harry automatically handed James five dollars; this was a trait that Glo had instilled in him. Not that he enjoyed hearing that Glo had gone down the hill. It could only mean that she was in the tavern, which was all there was down there. It was a sour little place that threw off a cold blue light at night. You could see the tops of people's heads in there and some shuffling around. Harry was curious about it, but it frightened him in the same way that the Catholic Church did. The tavern had always seemed out of place in a neighborhood in which most of the men took the subway to work in the morning and came home to eat dinner with their families at night. Harry hoped that Glo had not become a regular.

He sat on the metal railing in front of the pediatrician's office and waited for his mother. Harry and his family had been among the first tenants to rent an apartment in the building. The plaster was still wet when their moving van arrived. Harry was proud of his new address and would always work the conversation around so that he could mention it.

"I live in that new building on the hill," he would say. "How about you?"

The fact that it had an elevator was exciting too. He spent hours going up and down in it, pressing people's buttons for them as if he were a hired operator. Only later did he realize that some of those people might have enjoyed pressing their own buttons. He also loved having an incinerator instead of a dumbwaiter, although he was afraid of getting sucked up in it.

In the distance he saw Glo struggling up the hill. She had put on some weight and the expression on her face was a notch past cheeriness. In her excitement at seeing Harry, she fell to her knees, showing rolled-up stockings and a rooming-house leg. It was not the kind of homecoming Harry had in mind, but he ran over and picked her up and gave her a hug, anyway. Then the two of them went up to the old apartment together.

He had been out on the prairie and expected the place to seem smaller but not to have the walls crowd in on him to the extent that they did. But once he had put down his suitcase and hung his coat in the closet, he got accustomed to the narrow quarters. Before long, he was enjoying the snug fit of it.

While Glo was in the bedroom getting comfortable, Harry took a seat in the foyer and looked around. He concluded that the apartment still had the world's coziest lighting. Glo must have been a genius at it without even realizing it. One of the features that had appealed to Harry when they first moved in was the step-down living room. Each time Harry came home from school, he would step down into the living room and then step right up again. For old times' sake, he did it on this occasion and enjoyed it once again, although probably not as much. Harry then followed Glo into the bedroom with the idea of having a chat. He planned to ask her if he had made a mistake in not bringing home the lonely little Israeli and to sound her out on why he got a sinking feeling each time he thought about getting married—as beautiful as Sally was. But by the time he got in there, Glo was fast asleep, her big body half on and half off the bed. He hoisted her legs up and tried to make her more comfortable. He wasn't sure what he was loosening but guessed it was her stays.

Randy's bed was made up neatly beside Glo's as if it were

waiting for him to come back home and slip right in. Not for one second did Harry contemplate getting in there in place of his father, although it certainly would have been more comfortable than the living-room couch. He did take a peek inside Randy's closet, half expecting it to be filled up with suits. Harry at one time would go in there and stand in the middle of those suits for half an hour or so. He had spent quite a bit of his childhood standing in closets. But all that was in there now were a couple of ties, twisting on one end of a metal hanger. Randy had even taken along the hatboxes in which he kept his fedoras, as if to underscore the seriousness of his intentions.

After covering Glo with a blanket, Harry turned off the light and went back into the living room, where he lay down on the couch. You would think that he would be upset, what with Glo passed out in the bedroom, his father up the street with his mistress, and Sally thousands of miles away in the Midwest. But Harry was home and he felt fine.

Glo spent the next morning showing off Harry to her friends on the street.

"My kid just got out of the service," she said to a man who was sitting on a bench in front of the building, reading a newspaper. "He can barely fit his shoulders in the apartment."

"Good-looking boy," said the man, looking up from his newspaper for a moment and then returning to it.

Although Harry enjoyed being fawned over, he was starved and got Glo to have some breakfast with him in a luncheonette that had been carved out of a corner of their building. Harry recalled that none of its many owners had ever been able to make it profitable. A group that was described as being "a wonderful bunch of boys" would come in and try to make a go of it. When they failed, they would sell it to another even more wonderful bunch of boys who would do the same. The new owners were fat little brothers with black mustaches. Under their management, the orange juice seemed as fresh as ever; so were the eggs and the giant seeded rolls and butter. Although they seemed to be doing nicely, both had worried expressions on their faces.

Harry asked Glo what direction she felt he should take in looking for work. She said she believed the future lay in German delicatessens and that Harry should give some thought to opening one. If necessary, she would help out behind the counter.

"People are getting ready to forgive the Germans," said Glo. "And when they do, they are going to want to eat their coleslaw and potato salad."

Harry said he wasn't sure he wanted to go that way—but you never wanted to be too dismissive of Glo's theories—so he did say that he would keep an open mind.

In the Air Force, Harry had been classified, of all things, as an engineer. He had been put in charge of a gunnery range, his job being to fix up the targets so that they looked exactly like Korean villages. That way the pilots would feel they were blowing up the real thing. Harry had one hundred men under him and had gotten to be quite an expert on Korean artifacts, which he collected on buying trips to San Francisco. Harry and his men would place them about the range in what they thought was an authentic way; pilots who had already blown up actual villages in Korea swore they could not tell Harry's from the real thing. Many of them asked for Harry's targets personally. Despite this excellent showing, a career officer named Old Buss was slipped in over him. By his own admission, Old Buss did not know the first thing about targets, but he had suffered a hearing loss in combat and something had to be found for him. Harry didn't say anything and kept simulating his villages, but his heart was no longer in it. And when the time came to reenlist, he said no thanks, he would try his luck on the outside. He had the feeling that if he stayed in, there would always be an Old Buss being slipped in over him. Not that he had anything against Old Buss personally.

Harry could see that it was not going to be easy to apply the skills he had acquired in the Air Force to a job in civilian life. But while he was engaged in building targets for pilots to blow up, he found time to write a story about a fellow who did that very same thing, although he changed it around so that no one would think it was Harry. He showed it to his commanding officer, a towering Southerner who had read just about everything. Though his commanding officer did not comment on the story itself, he said that Harry certainly did look like a writer.

"When I saw you come through that door," he said, "I said to myself, shades of Dostoyevski."

It was not much to go on, but Harry thought he might take a crack at publishing.

He mentioned this to Glo in the luncheonette.

"It's a long shot," she said, "but do whatever makes you happy.

"And frankly," said Glo, "I would not mind having a job myself."

Harry let the remark go by. As much as he sympathized with Glo's situation, he was not about to package himself with his mother as a team. Although once he got established he would do everything he could to work her in. One of the men who had just taken over the luncheonette filled their coffee cups and went off to do the same for the two other customers. His brother wiped the counter until it sparkled, and arranged the Danish pastries so that they looked even tastier.

"They're such a wonderful bunch of boys," said Glo, shaking her head in amazement. "And they work so hard.

"But who knows if they can make a go of it."

After breakfast Harry set off down the street to see if he could round up some of his old friends. He had planned to take a nostalgic walk around the empty lot next door, perhaps recalling some of the great outfield catches he had made in it, but it had been filled in with an apartment building. A man came walking busily toward him, carrying a briefcase. He turned out to be Dartman, a once handsome boy with blue eyes and long lashes who had become bald overnight at the age of twelve. Harry had always wondered how he had handled his new situation.

"How are you, Dartman?" asked Harry.

"How *am* I?" asked Dartman, raising an eyebrow. "Good question. But first let's find out how you are."

"I'm fine," said Harry.

"Good," said Dartman. "Then I'm fine too."

With that he pursed his lips, batted his eyelashes, and continued his busy walk down the street. And Harry had his answer. Dartman's solution to his dilemma had been to read hidden meanings into the simplest of inquiries, bat his eyelashes, and keep moving. It seemed as good an approach as any.

In the store, Harry noted with disappointment that the new pharmacist had torn out the soda fountain and replaced it with racks of gift boxes of candy. On the counterman's day off Harry had once mixed a chocolate ice-cream soda for a man who had been a New York Yankee. He was nervous and probably botched it up, but the man who had been a New York Yankee had graciously said: "Nice soda, kid," and given him a dime. It wasn't that Harry yearned for a more innocent time. But he didn't see that gift boxes of candy represented the door to the future.

The pharmacist said that most of Harry's friends had moved out of the neighborhood and were practicing medicine in the Boston area. One had become a nurse, but even he had chosen to do his nursing in the Boston area. Though Harry was disappointed to hear this, he took comfort in knowing that if he was ever sick in the Boston area, there would be plenty of people to take care of him.

As if to contradict the pharmacist, a man entered the store who had been a marginal friend of Harry's. Pale and watery-eyed, Witz had slipped through neighborhood life without causing the least bit of commotion. Somehow Harry felt that he might have become a chiropodist, but he hadn't. Witz said that he had opened a clothing shop in midtown and seemed surprised that Harry was not about to do the same. But once he came to terms with Harry's decision not to open one, the two men shook hands with some passion. Unspoken was their joint commitment to do well in life, even though neither one was practicing medicine in the Boston area.

Only odd-lot type fellows seemed to have remained behind in the neighborhood. This probably meant that Harry was one, too, which did not bother him a bit. He felt loose and relaxed; after leaving the drugstore, he crossed the street and leapt up to catch the bottom rung of a fire-escape ladder, thinking he would do a few carefree swings on it. But the structure above began to tremble and he quickly dropped to the ground. That would have been something if he had pulled six fire-escape balconies down on his head. He realized that he had porked up quite a bit in the Air Force and considered going over to the track so he could start working it off. But he decided instead to see how his father was getting along. Randy's new apartment was only a city block away, but approaching it was like stepping out into Europe. The narrow streets gave way to an immense boulevard lined with trees and statuary that had indeed been brought over from Italy. It seemed to have been built to accommodate processions. Many older folks had been killed crossing this boulevard. Harry wondered if some of them hadn't stopped for a second to gaze at the enormous boulevard and not seen the oncoming cars.

Harry waited in the lobby while the doorman rang upstairs to see if it was all right to admit him. The lobby had white walls and maroon couches; it was quietly elegant, and Harry would have had no trouble moving right into the lobby itself and living there until he got his own place. Even though it was only a short ride and he was fresh and rested, Harry sat down on the bench in the elevator. It's here, he told himself. Why not use it. Trudy was waiting for him on the landing right outside the apartment. Never had Harry dreamed that he would have a father with a mistress and a landing outside his apartment. If he had been younger, he probably would have been shattered about the mistress, but as it was, he wasn't shattered.

Trudy gave him a hug and told him to come right in. Harry took a good look at Trudy and tried to see what it was in her that his father found appealing. It's true that she had straightened out his

115

business affairs and gotten him a position in a brokerage firm. But apart from that, all he saw was a small, bouncy-looking woman with a routine face. Her bathrobe was the same style as Glo's, but it was tailored to conform to the lines of her body. She seemed firm and bouncy in it. Maybe that's all there was to it. She had straightened out his affairs, and he liked to bounce around with her.

"You look wonderful," said Trudy. "The Air Force must have agreed with you."

"Thank you," said Harry. "I almost stayed in but decided not to."

Harry felt that Trudy was trying to win him over, which wasn't necessary. She went into the kitchen and came out with a sizzling plate of fat little steaks. Normally Harry would have been bowled over by their obvious juiciness and fine quality, but the Air Force had seen to it that Harry and his men had all the fat little steaks they wanted—as compensation for what was thought of as dangerous work. Actually it wasn't all that safe. Once you had set up your targets, it was important to get out of there quickly so that your ass did not get blown off by a low-flying bomber. And there were some Seminoles in the area who resented the Air Force using their land as a gunnery range. They would appear on a ridge from time to time and glare down at the targets. Harry could see their point of view; nonetheless, he and his men had to be on guard to repulse a possible attack by them. So maybe Harry deserved the fat little steaks, after all.

Since there was no point in wasting them, he dug into one of the steaks. As he did so, Randy shuffled out distractedly in his slippers. He seemed a bit taller, if such a thing were possible, and had developed a gently sloping paunch, which was encased in a monogrammed slipover sweater. He also had a brown and feathery little mustache. Harry would not have thought it possible, but he looked every bit the member of a brokerage firm. He had trouble meeting Harry's eyes and began to dance around on his toes, staying out of reach, as if he felt that Harry might strike out at him, which of course Harry had no intention of doing. He had been

116

careful not to be judgmental about Randy's abandonment of Glo.

But Randy himself seemed uneasy in the new situation. He began to dart in and out of his den, bringing out some of his acquisitions, such as cashmere sweaters in all colors and a set of scrimshaw knives.

"Take whichever one you like," he said, offering Harry one of the cashmeres.

Harry declined politely but said he would not mind having one of the scrimshaw knives.

"Not just now," said Randy, drawing them out of reach. "I'd like to hold on to those for a while."

After a period of continued awkwardness, they joined Randy's brother, Doug, who was watching a college football game on a tiny television set in the living room. Harry could barely make out the players, but it was the first time he had seen a television set in a private home. Harry was still marveling over pop-up toasters; now he was watching a ball game in an apartment. It seemed to Harry that science had stretched itself to its very limit and would have to take time out to regroup.

Doug was a jovial, thickset man who had prospered in the bathrobe industry although he never seemed to have an actual place of business. Harry had once accompanied him on his rounds. What he did was visit other bathrobe companies and do a lot of hearty laughing in the doorway of their showrooms. Harry had felt a little sorry for him not having a showroom of his own, until he learned that he had become enormously wealthy standing around in the doorways of other people's.

He and Randy had once fought nonstop for ten hours up and down the streets of lower Manhattan. They had not spoken to each other for twenty years after that, but they were speaking to each other now.

"You see those guys?" Doug said, pointing to the figures on the tiny TV screen. "I could lick the whole bunch of them, only make sure you don't tell them I said so. At least not until I'm on vacation."

117

With that he let out the hearty laugh that Harry remembered from the doorways of bathrobe companies. But there was a strain to it, as if he had begun to wonder why he had to be so hearty all the time.

He looked at Harry approvingly.

"The Air Force did quite a job on the kid, Randy," said the childless Doug, who never addressed Harry directly. "They must have fed him plenty of spinach."

"I have to whack off a few pounds," said Harry, patting his stomach.

"See that he doesn't whack off too much," Doug said to Randy. Then he sneaked a look at Trudy to make sure she hadn't picked up the innuendo.

"He's a big kid now," said Doug. "Has he got a girlfriend?"

"I believe so," said Randy. "What about that Harry?"

"I do," said Harry.

"That's too bad," said Doug. "I had a girl for him, except you don't want to be seen with her in the daylight."

His laugh was only semi-hearty, as if he were inching up on a more serious question.

"What's he think of McCarthy?" he asked Randy.

"Harry?"

"Not much," said Harry.

"Is that right," said Doug, sliding his chair over to Harry's and putting his jaw forward. "Well, here's what I think of him. I think he's the greatest thing to hit this country in a long time. You can take Adlai Stevenson and the rest of that crew and put them on a slow boat to Moscow. Because they stink to the high heavens."

"That's one way to look at it," said Trudy, turning to Harry as if she expected an eloquent reply from him. Though Harry was strongly opposed to his uncle's position, he had never been able to make such feelings known gracefully. His style was either to strike out physically at the other person or to cry out a strangulated word or two and then faint, which he did on this occasion.

When he came to, his head was against Trudy's bosom.

"What the hell happened here?" said Doug, standing over him. "I thought he was in the Air Force. What is he, a yellow belly or something?"

Harry looked at Randy and wondered if the two men were about to begin another ten-hour fighting session. When he saw that they weren't, he told his uncle to go fuck himself. Since he had already fainted, he felt he had nothing to lose.

"Now that's more like it," said Doug. "This is the kind of guy I could pal around with. What's he think of Israel?"

"I like it," said Harry, not waiting to be asked by his father.

"Now he's talking my language," said Doug, helping Harry to his feet. "Let me take him to the fights. We'll have a helluva time. I'd step into the ring myself except that they might not let me step out again. What do you say, Heshie?"

He let out his old doorway laugh but cut it off quickly when he saw that Trudy had stiffened at the use of Randy's old Lower East Side nickname.

"Oh, Jesus," said Doug, ducking down coyly and grabbing his coat. "I forget I'm not supposed to say 'Heshie' around here. I better get out before I catch the dickens."

When Doug had left, Randy looked at Harry squarely for the first time.

"That didn't upset you, did it?"

"Not really," said Harry.

"Because if it did, I'll say something to him. I'm not afraid of him."

"I know that. But it isn't necessary."

"All right, if you feel that way. But let me know if you change your mind."

Randy began to pace up and down again and to rearrange objects on an antique desk. Then he felt some cigars in a humidor to make sure they were soft. Finally Trudy handed him his overcoat and his briefcase and rang for the elevator.

Harry stayed behind to watch the end of the football game, examining the set greedily, as if he might never get a chance to watch another. On a chair beside him, Trudy crossed her plump legs and did some needlework. Her perfume would have been enticing if he had allowed it to be.

"Would you like some key-lime pie?" she asked.

"No thanks," said Harry.

"Is there anything I can get you?"

"I don't think so."

"Harry," she said.

"Yes."

"Your mother is a very beautiful woman."

"I know," said Harry.

Then he turned off the TV set, put his head against her neck, and cried for a while before he said good-bye.

Though he had fainted under the pressure of a right-wing attack and wept in the arms of his father's mistress, Harry felt surprisingly lighthearted as he crossed the sweeping boulevard once again. There seemed to be romance everywhere, and he was determined to have some for himself. Perhaps it was the effect on him of boulevards. In any case, he felt this was unfair to Sally and called her later that night, telling her how wonderful it was to be back in the city. If only she could be with him.

"But I *can* be with you," she said.

"Not until I have a job," he said, reminding her of their pact.

She asked him how he was coming along in his search for one, and Harry had to admit that he hadn't really gotten off the ground quite yet but that he was tooling up to do so.

"And I miss you very, very much," said Harry.

"I miss *you* very, very much," said Sally.

There were a great many very-verys in their subsequent conversation, and then it just petered out. That tended to happen with them. Sally had been one of the passengers on the streetcar that Harry crashed into when he first got the Chevy. She had taken it easy on him on the settlement, which is how they got to know each other. On dates they would talk about the interesting way they had met, and then the conversation would peter out. They slept together a few times, with Harry finding it pleasant and Sally finding it less so, although she did become aroused when there was a chance that someone might break in and catch them at it. But that petered out too. Harry liked taking pictures of Sally with her legs drawn back, exposing a slice of her panties. But there wasn't much more to it than that. Yet Harry was afraid he might never again get anyone so blond and pretty to pay attention to him. And Sally was one of the last of her girlfriends who was still unmarried. So they had become engaged and received a great many items of china, which were stored in crates behind a screen in the Turners' living room.

After they had hung up Harry took out one of the pictures he had taken of Sally with her legs drawn up and decided he was probably moving in the right direction. Still, he would not have minded talking over his confused feelings with Glo. But after making sure the apartment was immaculate, she had gone to bed early. On the kitchen table he found some travel brochures with a note saying that if Harry wanted to spend six months abroad, she would be happy to pay his expenses.

〜〜 THE FOLLOWING DAY HARRY PAID A visit to a few of the Manhattan buildings in which he felt it might be fun to work. Standing across the street from one of them, he saw people in the windows above holding clipboards and chewing speculatively on pencils. Suddenly he longed to be holding one of those clipboards and chewing speculatively on one of those pencils. But he could not think of anyone who would be helpful in getting him started. His Uncle Doug knew only right-wing radio announcers and owners of bathrobe companies. Glo's friends, for the most part, were usherettes. And Randy seemed to be good only for concerned looks. As a graduate of a mining school, Harry would have been in a good situation if he had set his sights on metallurgy. But the only graduate of the school who had gone on to prominence in the media was Newt Lowry, who had become a famed network-time salesman. Known to be a generous man, Newt had helped more than one graduate of the school to make the switch from mining to network-time sales. But there was just so much he could do without endangering his own job. Harry did not feel it was fair to add to Newt's burden. Somehow he would have to slip into the field on his own.

At noontime Harry walked into the lobby of one of the buildings he'd admired and entered a stream of workers to try to get the feel of what it would be like to have a job and be going out to lunch. Two sandy-haired men who were his own age and carried brief-cases and umbrellas gave him sharp looks, as if they had caught him trying to blend in. When most of the workers had gone, Harry introduced himself to a tall, distinguished-looking black man who appeared to be the uniformed lobby supervisor and asked if he knew of any jobs that were available. The supervisor, who could not have been nicer, said that he didn't know of any at the moment but that he would certainly keep his ear to the ground. Harry thanked him and decided to pack it in for the day, having concluded that there was no point in going all out on his first try.

On an impulse he decided to call Robert Appleman, who had been the bow-and-arrow instructor at Harry's summer camp and was the most interesting person he knew. Everything about Appleman was interesting except his appearance, which was not that interesting. He was plump and of medium height, with a flush to his cheeks that may or may not have been related to good health. On the first day of the season they had gotten into a playful scuffle, with Appleman suddenly drawing back and saying it would not be a good idea to continue, since he might have to kill Harry, which would be a simple matter for him. Though Harry felt he was stronger than Appleman, there was something about the way he delivered the warning and his accompanying chuckle that made Harry decide not to challenge him. At the age of sixteen Appleman had already taken advanced courses in psychology at New York University and was headed smartly in the direction of a career as a psychoanalyst.

Though Appleman showed little interest in dating, he had pulled off a tremendous feat by seducing the head of the girls' camp in her tub on the last day of the season. Harry was sick when he heard about it. Though the woman had the best body in camp, she came off as a serious individual who drank hot water and lemon for breakfast and took solitary canoe trips on her days off. No one even knew she was interested in sex. Except, of course, for Appleman, who, with his knowledge of psychology, had spotted something.

Though Harry had been envious of Appleman's triumph, he continued to be fond of his plump and affable friend and was delighted to find him at home.

Appleman agreed to have dinner with Harry and suggested that they meet at an obscure fish restaurant that was a favorite of his.

The two men embraced on meeting, Harry doing so cautiously since he did not want Appleman to mistake his intentions and kill him. After cocktails Harry followed his friend's lead and ordered a turtle steak. The meat was routine in taste, but Harry enjoyed the idea of it and was happy to see that Appleman had remained true to form in suggesting a fascinating dinner. He anticipated that his friend would have some tasty new caper to tell him about, and he was not disappointed. Appleman had spent the summer as an attendant in the violent ward of a mental institution. As one of his duties, he had been put in charge of a ninety-year-old man who was attached to life-support equipment. On a whim, Appleman had decided to turn it off.

"Holy shit," said Harry, making no attempt to be casual. "What did you do that for?"

"I couldn't help it," said Appleman with a self-effacing chuckle. "He was going to die, anyway. It was irresistible, having all that power in my hands."

Harry hardly knew how to respond to this. What struck him is how little outrage he felt. If decency required that he storm out of the fish restaurant, he failed the test miserably. It wasn't that he admired Appleman for his actions. But he could not help but be impressed.

Apart from his target-range work and his engagement to Sally, the best Harry could come up with at his end was a skirmish with a corset model in a roadhouse outside Denver. At that, he had to dress up the episode to make it presentable. After he had listened to Harry's story, Appleman snuffled graciously through his nose. It was an engaging mannerism, and once again Harry was filled with admiration for his intriguing friend, who had been able to turn a simple sinus condition into a strength. No doubt it was the kind of thing that had helped him to charm his way into the head counselor's tub.

Midway along in their dinner, Harry became aware of a handsome, gray-haired man at the next table. He had kept his hat on through dinner and had been reading a furled-up journal. And he, too, had ordered the turtle steak. At one point he smiled at Appleman, who smiled back. The two men lifted their forks and waved a bite of turtle at one another, inclining their heads as if in mutual appreciation of the delicacy. Harry speared a bite of his own and attempted to join in, but by the time he did, the two men had set down their forks.

Before long, Appleman and the man struck up a conversation that quickly took a turn toward the psychological, with references to the id and superego being bandied about freely. Though the man, who was either a psychiatrist or a student of the subject, was clearly in his fifties, Appleman not only held his own with him but led the discussion into fresh areas, such as astrology and Zoroastrianism. So stimulating was the exchange that the two had soon exchanged phone numbers and agreed to have another at the man's Fifth Avenue home. Though Harry enjoyed reading case histories of deranged people, he had barely been able to follow a word they were saying and felt terribly left out. He considered trying to work in his knowledge of the Balkans but could not find a suitable opening and decided not to try to force it in.

Soon after the man had left, Appleman and Harry were joined by a tall, rangy girl who sat on the edge of her chair and with barely a glance at Harry began dramatically to sweep one hand back through her long black hair. Appleman introduced her as his friend Daphne and was able to hold her in check for a while with his engaging nose snuffles. When her restlessness got out of hand, Appleman rose from his chair and, with his napkin still stuck in his belt, led Harry aside to an alcove. There he asked if Harry would be kind enough to excuse him for the evening since he and his friend had made a date to go back to his room and do some farting under the covers.

"Oh, Jesus," said Harry in what had become his standard response to Appleman's shockers.

But then he collected himself and told Appleman it was perfectly all right and to go on ahead and not worry about him. When the couple had left, Harry told the waitress to take away the uneaten part of the turtle steak. And to bring him a check. He considered the evening. Once again his friend had amazed him by cheerfully admitting to a murder and then casually making friends with a sophisticated man who was easily thirty years his senior. And now there was the daring new dating activity. The idea of even farting once and having a pretty girl be aware of it was unthinkable. Yet here was his friend who was about to make it the centerpiece of an entire evening. Harry thought about it for a while and decided that in this one instance his friend had been too fascinating.

After a week of examining the outsides of buildings and peering in at outer offices, Harry decided it was time for him to focus on the actual business of getting a job. Since his only significant contact had been with the kindly lobby supervisor, he decided to drop around to see him one morning after first stopping to buy him a pound of cookies.

The supervisor thanked him for his thoughtfulness.

"I don't eat sweets, but if it's all right with you, I'll take them home for my wife."

Harry lingered for a bit in the lobby and learned that his new friend, whose name was Dandy Boisseau, was a painter, and that his brother, a novelist, taught a highly regarded course in fiction in Greenwich Village.

"What would you think about taking it?" asked the supervisor. "It's generally oversubscribed, but Carl has never turned me down on a recommendation."

Since his prospects were dim at the moment and he wasn't entirely clear on whether he wanted actually to have a job, Harry did not see how he could go wrong in taking up the kind offer.

"Maybe I can get him in now," said Boisseau. "Do you happen to have a dime?"

Harry gave him one and watched his friend go off across the lobby and insert it in the pay phone.

"It's all set," said Boisseau after making the call. "As it happens, Carl had a cancellation and will be happy to put you in. He asks only that you bring along a sample of your output."

"You're sure you're not going out on a limb?" said Harry. "I don't have much."

He told him about his Korean target work.

"Sounds to me like it's right on the money."

It occurred to Harry that black men had always come along to help him at critical junctures in his life. On the day that he'd suddenly decided to pack up and leave the Idaho School of Mines, it was a black railroad conductor who had bought him a sandwich and suggested he give it another try. And now it was happening again, with Dandy Boisseau virtually materializing out of nowhere in a lobby to give him a boost. Lobbies had been lucky for him as well.

"I really do appreciate this," said Harry. "Is there anything I can do for you? For example, would you and the wife care to see a musical?"

"That's very kind," said Boisseau. "But actually there's nothing on the boards at the moment that interests us. Should you ever rise to prominence, I'll let you come back and purchase one of my oils."

That night Harry called Sally, who reported that the last of her girlfriends had gotten married.

"You remember Tammy," said Sally. "The one whose left breast is much smaller than her right one?"

Harry said he did remember her although he had never been able to keep her breasts straight. He told her about the course he was about to take; Sally, registering neither approval nor disappointment, said that her picture was being used to help promote bus travel.

They agreed that it was nice that Harry was taking his course and that Sally's picture was being used to help promote bus travel.

Suddenly Harry felt that he was losing her and flailed around desperately to find some common ground.

"Do you still like Frank Sinatra?" he asked finally.

"Yes," said Sally.

"So do I," said Harry with passion and relief. "I like him more than ever."

The silence that followed was unbearable. During their courtship they had assigned pet names of a coy nature to their private parts. He decided to try a daring gambit.

"How is your toosie?" he asked.

"Fine," said Sally.

"Great," said Harry. "So is my pippy."

Feeling that the exchange had brought them somewhat closer together, Harry said good-bye and that he missed her very, very much. She said that she missed him, too, but the connection was a poor one and he could not say for sure that she had added very, very much.

PROFESSOR CARL BOISSEAU WAS A tall, sparse-haired man who was every bit as distinguished-looking as his brother, Dandy, but whose manner ran more to the austere. Harry quickly learned from a fellow student that he had written a well-received Dust Bowl novel and then lapsed into a mysterious fictional silence, surfacing after many years as the teacher of his successful course. Several graduates had gone on to publish novels of their own with one of them unaccountably returning to the class that Harry had just joined. A lean, sandy-haired man, he sat close to Professor Boisseau, his legs crossed at the ankles, and used the phrase *sort of* whenever he was called upon for comments. Harry was instantly enamored of him and kept sneaking glances in his direction.

The class was every bit as popular as Dandy Boisseau had indicated. Each seat was filled; Harry had seen Professor Boisseau in the corridor, accepting applications from students who hoped for cancellations. Harry was all the more grateful to Dandy Boisseau for sponsoring him and was anxious to make a good showing. More than half of the students were men in denim jackets whose works concerned the rigors of war. They sat slumped over expressionlessly in their seats, as if they were being carried off to battle. There were many attractive women in the group, some of whom came across as housewives and young mothers. On closer inspection, one of the women turned out to be Appleman's friend Daphne. She wore a white silk blouse and black pajama pants and seemed as restless as ever, stretching her long legs out and, in what Harry saw as a trademark gesture, running her hands back through

129

her long black hair. Considering the circumstances of their last meeting, Harry was not entirely sure he wanted to see her, although the night with Appleman appeared to have left her untouched. Additionally, he had not been aware that her legs were quite that long.

Professor Boisseau got each class under way by reading from the work of one of the students, whose identity was kept a secret. The class was then invited to throw off criticisms, with Boisseau coming in, when these tailed off, to knit them together in a common thread. The pieces were given full dramatic presentations, with Boisseau acting out each of the characters and switching over to falsetto for the female roles. Sounds of battle were simulated effectively with deep rumbling noises. Harry enjoyed the readings, treating them as if they were a stage show and forgetting for the most part that he was in a classroom. When called upon for comment, he was careful to find merit in each of the selections and never to be discouraging.

Midway along in the second week, Professor Boisseau led off with a piece that dealt with a young girl's thoughts as she slid across a kitchen floor on imaginary skates and examined the reflection of her vagina on the linoleum floor. Harry found the piece powerfully erotic and could not believe one of the women in the room had written it. Sight unseen, he felt he was willing to run off with her. As Boisseau warmed to his dramatization, it was all Harry could do to keep from asking to be excused so that he could relieve himself in the corridor. There was silence in the room when the reading was concluded and the sense that its content had struck home with many in the group. The first to speak was a denim person who, in an attempt to be waggish, commented tastelessly on the story's "topography" and was quickly hooted down. Other class members arose to treat the work soberly, all being in agreement that a delicate topic had been handled with sensitivity.

Professor Boisseau next did a selection that sounded curiously familiar to Harry, who soon realized that he had written it. There was something voyeuristic about having his own work read aloud with no one but Boisseau aware of his identity. Harry slumped down in his chair; it was all he could do to keep his composure. Professor Boisseau's rendition of Harry's main character seemed strained; Harry felt the emphasis had been put in the wrong places. But Boisseau's dramatization of the Seminole women and their keening, heart-rending cries when they first set eyes upon the gunnery range was fresh and unexpected. When the brief reading was concluded, bland comments were made to the effect that the author, with seeming accuracy, had thrown light on a little-known aspect of the military. Professor Boisseau next called upon a stocky man with a beret who got to his feet and denounced the work as being sick.

"It's not just the characters and the situation," said the man. "I suppose I could live with just that. But it's the whole bloody sensibility of the piece. For God's sake, the man's even succeeded in having the poor Seminoles come off as being a neurotic tribe. I'm surprised that all of you can just sit here and let that go by. This is a sick piece by a sick man. Sick, sick, sick."

The man directed a long, slow scowl at the class in general, as if waiting for a challenge. When none was offered, he sat down disgustedly, snapped open a newspaper, and buried his head in it.

"I sort of see what you're driving at," said the published man after a moment of strain. "But aren't you sort of exaggerating just a tad?"

"No, you idiot," said the man in the beret, looking up from his newspaper. "I'm holding back."

"Now look here," said the published author, uncrossing his ankles. "I'm sort of getting ticked off."

There was a sense that the two men might very well fly at each other. Responding to this possibility, the denim people lumbered forward and took up strategic positions close by. At that point Professor Boisseau stepped in and calmed the class. He reminded everyone of his policy of keeping students' identities a secret but suggested that in this one case it might be useful for the author, if he were willing to do so, to remove his or her mask.

131

"And I urge you do this," said Boisseau, looking out above Harry's head so as not to give him away, "and to enlighten us, if you will, as to what on God's earth you're driving at."

"Gladly," said Harry, getting nimbly to his feet and without realizing it going over to Boisseau's falsetto. "In truth, I don't have anything in particular in mind. What I thought I'd do is sort of mosey along for a bit and see where it all takes me."

It was Harry's first use of the phrase *sort of,* which he found bracing.

"And incidentally," he said, turning to the man in the beret, as if in conclusion. "I don't find the work anywhere near as sick as you do. Not by a long shot. No, sir."

"Excellent," said the man with a dismissive wave. "That's your opinion."

"It certainly is," said Harry. "And what's your opus about, pray tell?"

He looked at the class as if to say, "This is going to be good."

"The cosmos," said the man loftily.

"Oh, wonderful," said Harry. "And I suppose that's not sick."

"It's as healthy as a newborn," said the man.

Seemingly unruffled, he returned to his newspaper, laughing heartily at its contents.

"We'll see about that," said Harry, who suddenly became light-headed and found his collar tightening in a vise. At that point he pitched forward and fainted.

When he came to, he saw that he was in the corridor, with Daphne kneeling beside him and splashing his face with water from a nearby drinking fountain.

"Are you all right?" she asked.

"Fine," said Harry, who was surprised that he had fainted, since he felt he had been doing nicely in the exchange. But evidently he'd been much more upset than he realized. Hearing his work criticized publicly had been devastating. And it was disappointing to have fainted for the second time since he'd become a civilian.

Obviously, if this was his way of dealing with adversity, he had a long, hard road ahead of him.

"It's none of my business," said Daphne, "but they were terribly unfair to you."

"Really," said Harry with nonchalance. "In what sense?"

"Come, come," she said with impatience. "It was my vagina story that was read."

"It was?" said Harry, reviving quickly.

"Yes," she said. "So I know what you're going through."

"But they loved your work."

"Oh, yes," she said, "I suppose they found their own lurid little reasons for embracing it—missing the metaphor entirely, of course—but they'll catch up with me in due course. On the other hand, you're so sweet and kind and vulnerable, they felt they had the perfect target. They set out to hurt you terribly, and they succeeded, didn't they? They always do."

"Maybe yes and maybe no," said Harry. "But there's no way I'm going back there."

"Nor should you," said Daphne, helping him to his feet. "But you're safe now and we're going to take very, very good care of you."

"Just out of curiosity," said Harry, "a metaphor for what?"

"For torrid sex," she said with a growl. "Now come along. We're going to begin your convalescence with pots and pots of lovely, lovely coffee."

Though Harry was a milk drinker, he allowed himself to be led off.

The café to which Daphne took him was filled with attractive young people wearing the insignia of nearby universities and carrying on conversations that buzzed with artistic concerns. Harry longed to be one of them but felt handicapped by his attendance at a mining school. Then, too, the talk was all of Greek classics, while Harry's strength was in Balkan feuds.

He thought he might as well get the troubling Appleman connection cleared up as quickly as possible.

"Oh, God," she said, her face coloring. "I can just about imagine what the little monster told you. You'll have to take my word for it that it's all nonsense."

Harry said he was relieved and that it was the particular nature of the activity Appleman had described that had thrown him off.

"Let's just put it out of our minds, shall we," said Daphne.

"And suppose, in theory, that it was true," she said, switching gears. "Can't we consider it a phase? You'll grant that our Freudian friend has charm, *n'est-ce pas?*"

"Absolument," said Harry, whose school of mines happily had insisted on one semester of language. "He's the most interesting guy I've ever met."

"And you, my darling, are the sweetest. We're going to see lots and lots of each other. And somehow—though I haven't devised my diabolical plan just yet—I plan to spirit you away to Paris. You can do your work while I sit at your feet, and when you've finished for the day, there'll be extraordinary wine and I'll cook for you, though I'm afraid I'll make a hash of it at first . . . so you'll have to be patient with me, my darling . . . and there'll be walks in the rain, sad ones, I should imagine, and, of course, hours and hours of lovely, lovely love. . . ."

Her voice had become husky and there was a catch to it, as if she were on the verge of tears. Harry found her style outrageously mannered but he enjoyed it all the same and had to wonder if that is what he had been seeking in the city—outrageous mannerism. He thought of Sally, and the concern must have shown on his face.

"Hush, my darling," she said, putting a finger to his lips before he could speak. "There's no need to explain. Of course there's someone, and why shouldn't there be? Wouldn't it be a lovely surprise for me if there weren't? I'm envious, of course, but at the same time I take my hat off to the little vixen. She must be very clever indeed."

134

"It's just someone I'm a little engaged to," said Harry.

"I'm sure she's terribly special," said Daphne, whose hands shook and who seemed genuinely upset. "Now, if you don't mind, my sweet, I'd like to finish my coffee and savor the precious time that's been granted to me."

"To us," said Harry, correcting her and feeling as if he were an old Frenchman and there was no need to go to Paris.

"You're very dear," said Daphne with fatalism, "but I'm afraid I had it right the first time."

Daphne lived with her family in a dark, baronial apartment building overlooking the Hudson. Harry drove her home. They parked on a nearby bluff. The day previous, there had been no romance in his life. Now it seemed there was more than he could handle.

Daphne was not as pretty as Sally, but she was almost as pretty, and there were the legs and the catch in her voice. Harry could not get enough of what his favorite novelist of the period would have called her phoniness. It did not bother him. He felt there was sincerity beneath it. And what if there weren't? What if she were entirely phony? Thank God for phoniness, he declared to himself as he kissed her. He thought of her vagina story, which he felt he could recite after the one hearing, and plunged his hand beneath her skirt. She caught it gently at the wrist, but not before it had brushed against the most delicate and no doubt expensive underwear he had ever touched. . . .

"Not just yet, my darling," she said. "You can have me, of course, and you know that. You must have known the moment we set eyes on each other. . . ."

"At the fish restaurant?"

"No, no, darling, I don't count that. Tonight. But if you can bear it, I'd like it to happen at the right time. When I give myself to you, and I shall, my sweet, I can assure you of that, I want it to be unlike anything experienced before by two people in the cosmos."

135

"Don't say *cosmos.*"

"Sorry, darling. And I do so want you to meet daddoo."

The following night, Harry dined with Daphne and her family in the lugubrious dining room of their dark and drafty apartment. Despite the dank atmosphere, there was a hint of wealth in the air although it was difficult to determine just how much. Seated alongside Mr. Kravitz was a plump Indian woman in a sari who was his fourth wife and who looked at her husband quizzically throughout the meal. This last marriage had lasted longer than the previous ones, perhaps owing to the quizzical looks. Harry was surprised that he was able to eat with such relish. He had always done so sparingly at girlfriends' houses, thinking it would be rude to put a strain on the family budget. He decided that it was his experience in the armed forces that had hardened him.

"Harry plans to become a writer," said Daphne.

"You know what I think of them," said the tall and dour Mr. Kravitz.

"What might that be?" asked Harry.

"Shits if you ask me."

Though he was annoyed by Mr. Kravitz's remark, Harry counted it as a victory that he had not fainted. The Indian woman looked at her husband more quizzically than she had previously.

"Surely not all of them," said Harry.

"Every bloody one."

"Certainly not Harry's kind," said Daphne.

"His certainly," said Mr. Kravitz, refusing to budge.

"Besides," added Daphne, fudging a bit, "Harry's father is in your line."

"Wall Street?" said Mr. Kravitz, perking up. "What name does he go by?"

"Randy Towns," said Harry. "And he doesn't go by it. That's his name."

"Oh, that shark," said Mr. Kravitz with a harsh laugh. "I should have known."

"Now look here," said Harry. "Randy Towns doesn't have a mean bone in his body."

Though slightly angry, he couldn't help but be pleased to hear his father, who had been thought of by many as being ineffectual, described as a shark.

"Not the Randy Towns I know."

"Then obviously it's a mistake," said Harry, wondering if Mr. Kravitz hadn't seen a side of his father that had escaped him.

"Oh, don't misunderstand," said Mr. Kravitz. "I wouldn't mind being a double-dealer myself. I'd have gotten a lot farther. But I'm just not built that way."

"Few of us are," said Harry, who realized that his rejoinder had little sting to it. He was able to see why Mr. Kravitz had experienced marital difficulties.

Daphne, on the other hand, had turned out nicely, so perhaps her father had attractive qualities that hadn't surfaced at the dinner table. Harry asked him what he had against writers.

Mr. Kravitz laughed bitterly and then led Harry to the living room, where he produced a well-thumbed volume that fell open easily to a circled passage.

"Read that," said Mr. Kravitz, "if you have the stomach for it."

Harry whipped through the offending paragraphs, which dealt with a dwarf who runs a coffeehouse in Vienna and treats his clientele rudely.

"I'm afraid I don't follow," said Harry.

"A man who pretended to be my father's best friend wrote it," Daphne explained. "He feels it's a thinly disguised portrait of him."

"Heavily, if you ask me," said Harry.

"No one asked you," said Mr. Kravitz.

"Daddoo."

"Oh, for God's sakes, Daphne," said Mr. Kravitz, "anyone with a brain in his head can tell it's me who is being ridiculed. Anyone who knew me then, anyone who knows me now. Anyone with eyes.

"And I've had to deal with the disgrace all these years. Antholo-

137

gies, fresh new editions. And it's not over yet. Wait and see, they'll be reprinting this bloody libel until I'm in the grave.

"And that's what you fellows do," said Mr. Kravitz, burying his head in his hands.

Mrs. Kravitz comforted her husband and then led Daphne and Harry into the study.

"Think of the whole," she said. "Never the parts."

Harry found the advice mundane, but he was happy that she had at least passed along something, since he'd been hoping for a few of her Far Eastern insights.

"Thank you, my precious," said Daphne, kissing her step-mother on the cheek.

Turning to Harry, she said, "Malati has never once failed us."

≈≈ HARRY WAS ANXIOUS TO BE ALONE with Daphne, but since he had no idea of how to deal with hotels, they went back to the bluff and sat in the car, looking down at the Hudson River.

"He admires you," said Daphne. "It's so classic, two headstrong bulls facing each other down, neither willing to give ground. But he'll come around, I assure you."

"I can't stop thinking of that vagina story of yours," said Harry in a sweeping change of topic.

"The symbolism?" said Daphne.

"No, the actual thing that happens."

"Oh, that," said Daphne offhandedly. "But you know I'd be happy to reenact it for you, if it would give you the slightest bit of pleasure."

"It would, actually," said Harry, "but there's no need to go to all that trouble."

He wondered where he had picked up the habit of saying the opposite of what he meant. And when he would begin doing the reverse. Probably never was his gloomy conclusion.

Daphne stretched out her long legs and put her hands behind her head, which gave her smallish breasts some prominence.

"Would you make love to me, my darling? I'm ready now, you know."

"Sure," said Harry.

He kissed her, for appearance's sake, and then plunged his hand beneath her skirt, withdrawing it immediately.

"What's wrong?" she asked.

"You're all wet."

139

"That's because I'm ready."

"It is?" said Harry, who had always thought of this state as representing a finale.

"You poor sweet darling, you don't know a thing, do you?"

"I wouldn't go that far."

"It's not your fault. You were probably never given a saucy nanny to instruct you."

Harry was slightly annoyed and pointed out that a black woman had looked after him from time to time—although he had to concede that the three-hundred-pound Clara had not been saucy.

"Well, then, we'll just have to begin at the beginning."

Dutifully Harry allowed her to guide his hand beneath her skirt once again.

"Higher," said Daphne.

"Higher than this?" said Harry.

"Oh, yes, much higher."

"How's that?"

"That's not quite it," said Daphne.

After several more tries Harry said that although he meant no disrespect, he didn't see how he could possibly go any higher.

"Very well, then," she said, kissing him sweetly. "We'll just have to make do."

Harry made love to her and discovered there was much more to it than he had realized. In the case of Sally, he had generally retired after a thrust or two, leaping to his feet and saying: "That about does it, I guess." Daphne shifted her position often and seemed to enjoy it enormously, helping to wrap up matters with a great spidery maneuver that Harry found pleasurably devouring.

"Well," said Daphne, stretching out her legs luxuriously and resting her head on the seat. "There's no question you've some aptitude for this. And it's a good thing you didn't get an early start. You might have become unbearable. Can we try it again, my darling?"

Harry was puzzled by the request and said he didn't see much point to it. He realized that he may have come across as being snappish and apologized—but by that time they were on their way to the apartment. The Kravitzes had retired. There was a smell of incense in the air. Harry followed Daphne into the kitchen, where she busied herself making chicken sandwiches. When they were ready, she put them on a tray and glided across the linoleum floor to deliver them.

"Oh, my God," said Harry as the reading in Boisseau's class came back to him. He took the tray away from her and ended up trying it again, after all.

Harry felt awful about betraying Sally and thought it best to make a clean breast of it as soon as possible. He called her that night and said he was afraid he'd gotten in a bit over his head with a fellow student. Sally said that was odd, since she had gotten in over her head with the man who had used her photograph to promote bus travel.

"How far over your head are you?" asked Harry, who found that he was suddenly shaken.

"I'm not sure," said Sally. "It all happened late at night in one of the buses."

"Is it over?" asked Harry.

He felt there was a good chance he would go into a third and possibly final faint.

"It's hard to tell," said Sally.

"Well, mine's over," said Harry, "so how can you say that yours isn't?"

"It probably is," said Sally. "It's just that I'm not sure."

They ended the conversation weakly at that point, with Harry concluding that it would be wise for him to get a job as soon as possible.

He saw Daphne in broad daylight for the first time the following afternoon. Her skin was pale, and as she watched him approach, her legs became unsteady and she clutched at a railing. He ran to her and had to hold her to keep her from falling. When she had

141

regained her balance, they had a drink at a nearby café. Though Harry knew little about wine, he did not feel that the one they had chosen was extraordinary.

"It's over, isn't it," said Daphne.

"I did sort of speak to Sally last night."

Now that Harry had begun to use the phrase *sort of,* he found it difficult to keep it out of conversations.

"It's all right, my darling," she said, lighting a cigarette and taking a hungry puff as if it were her last. "I'm going to be fine. I'll try to be brave, of course, but I can't guarantee that I'm not going to cry and be sad for an absurdly long time. But do go on about your life. You mustn't alter it a bit. And one day, my darling, when I'm at my most despairing, I'm going to wake up and square my shoulders and see the bright blue sky and realize that it's going to be all right, after all, and that perhaps it wasn't totally foolish of me to fall in love with an unbearably attractive young man named Harry Towns."

Holding a handkerchief to her nose, she began to cry right then. Though she had been at her most actressy, the tears were almost certainly real, and Harry felt awful when he backed out of the café. He had slept with her and enjoyed it enormously, but he had slept with Sally first and he didn't have the faintest idea of how you went about breaking off an engagement. Besides, Daphne showed every evidence of caring for him, which was confusing. The wisest course seemed to be to end their affair immediately.

Soon afterward Harry received a letter from Professor Carl Boisseau saying that he understood entirely Harry's decision not to continue with the class.

"As a young man, I had a similar urge," wrote Boisseau, "and only wish that I'd found the courage, as you have, to stop writing while there was still time."

Though Harry was disappointed by the contents of the letter, he was pleased that Boisseau had taken the time to write to him instead of simply filling Harry's seat as if he had never been in it.

THE CURRENT CLIMATE

He was determined, nonetheless, to prove the professor wrong, and continued, each morning, to try to push back the boundaries of his target story. This was difficult, since it had been declared sick; nonetheless, he persisted.

Nor did Harry forget his pledge to try to get a job so that he and Sally could get married. Through an usherette friend of Glo's, he was hired briefly to do promotional work on a Broadway show that closed just as he had gotten the hang of publicity releases. The producer graciously paid him a week's salary, which he took out of the folds of his cloak. Soon afterward Harry received a job offer from a magazine that dealt with fireplace ornaments but backed off when told he would be expected to attend cross-dressing parties on Long Island. An executive at a wire service said that he had no openings at the moment but encouraged Harry to read a piece that he had written on the subject of garlic. Harry whipped through it at a nearby restaurant and found it instructive, although he could not honestly say that it had pointed him in some bold new direction. It did have the effect of sharpening his appetite for spicy foods, and he was happy to see that goulash was on the menu.

At no point did Harry become discouraged. He felt that, magically, something would come up. Hadn't the Idaho School of Mines opened its doors to him when nine other colleges had turned him down? And what about the Air Force, plucking him out of a large group of new arrivals and asking him to design targets that resembled the Korean countryside?

In the meanwhile Harry settled into his old apartment and enjoyed lazy days and some of the finest naps he had ever taken. Each morning, after a session on his target yarn, he set out in the direction of a giant milk-bottle display that sat atop the headquarters of a far-off dairy company. Though he never quite made it to the bottle, which seemed to recede as he drew near, he enjoyed striking out in the direction of it. He discovered an out-of-the-way little movie house that showed European films that were new to him, such as *The Loves of Gosta Berling* and *The Cabinet of Dr. Caligari*. Sitting among hawk-nosed men in oversize topcoats, he

143

felt pleasantly dislocated, as if he were a young man living in Prague. From time to time he had dinner with Travis, who had been a friend at the Idaho School of Mines and recently had returned from medical school in France after a year of not understanding a single word of the instruction. Travis, who had been a cheerleader at school, turned mournful the day he graduated and had never recovered from either his campus celebrity or a series of failed romances with identical-looking blond farm girls. After dinner, as they walked through the park, Travis would suddenly drop to his knees and do silent mining-school cheers, as if he were in an abandoned stadium. It was Travis's plan to strike out for the West and try his hand at pharmaceuticals.

In many ways it was a carefree and happy time for Harry, and although there was no question that he would honor his engagement to Sally, he often wished that he could continue on as he was indefinitely. A cheerful note in his life was that a change had come over Glo. She had stopped wearing her bathrobe and slippers in the street and switched over to brightly colored, freshly starched housedresses. The puffiness had disappeared from her face, allowing her cheekbones to reappear along with the slightly uneven smile he had always admired. She let her hair get gray, which was a shock to Harry at first. But he quickly became accustomed to it, preferring it to the henna color that was neither here nor there. There was a peaceful look in her eyes that concerned him, but he tried to ignore it.

One day she asked Harry what he would think about taking her downtown for lunch and a Broadway show. He jumped at the chance; it had been one of his favorite things to do when he was growing up, but they hadn't had that kind of day since he had gotten out of the armed forces.

Glo wore a conservative blue suit for the excursion, one that she kept pressing down to make sure it fit smoothly around the hips. She asked him what he thought of the trimming, and he said it looked fine although, in truth, he had never been that interested in trimming. Before they left, she pulled the collar of her blouse down and exposed her neck, asking Harry if he thought she had on too much perfume. He said she seemed to have on just the right amount.

They looked for a cab on the boulevard and were able to flag one down right beneath the window of Randy's luxurious apartment. On the ride downtown, Harry expected that at any moment Glo would begin to talk to the driver and would end up knowing his whole life story, and the driver knowing hers. But she didn't say a word. She just looked out of the window with the peaceful look that he had found troubling.

The play they saw had to do with six performers sitting around in a living room and discussing a fascinating man who had died just before the action began. Harry would have preferred that the play had started a little earlier so that you could actually meet the fascinating man instead of just hearing about him. But he assumed the play sponsors knew what they were doing. And he enjoyed it all the same. It starred Katharine Cornell—Glo called her Kit Cornell—and when it was over, Glo contended that it was Kit Cornell who had carried the play. Harry agreed that she had been wonderful but felt that the author had something to do with the success of the work as well.

"It isn't easy to keep your attention for two hours talking about someone who's just dropped dead," he said.

"That may be so," said Glo. "But I don't think they would have gotten to first base if they didn't have Kit Cornell in it."

They had a spirited argument about this on the way to Sardi's, with Glo more than holding her own. Harry enjoyed her not giving in to him just because he was her son, although he would have preferred that she not call the actress Kit Cornell.

The restaurant was emptying out when they got there, and they were given a choice booth along the wall. Harry enjoyed sitting in it, even though he knew it would have been assigned to luminaries if it had been a peak hour. Harry scanned the menu and asked Glo what she felt like eating. But she seemed more interested in who was in the restaurant than what was on the menu. She poked Harry in the ribs, drawing his attention to a trim, distinguished-looking man with a neat little mustache who was being helped into his coat by the captain. It was a camel's-hair coat with a fur collar. When the man had his coat on, the captain clicked his heels, did a little bow, and handed him his homburg hat. Glo said the man was a producer of dozens of Broadway shows, including the one they had just seen that had Kit Cornell in it. She said he was quite a man. Normally, in that situation, Glo would have gone over to the producer, introduced herself, and told him all about her son Harry back there in the booth. She didn't do that on this occasion, which made Harry all the more concerned about the peaceful look in her eyes. For the first time he got angry at Randy for living up the street with a hot little schnitzel. He felt like finding him and dragging him over to Sardi's to see what had happened to Glo and to ask him what he planned to do about it. After all, he had started the goddamned family. Shouldn't he finish it? Instead he excused himself and walked up to the producer.

"Excuse me, sir," said Harry, trying to control his anger. "My mother isn't feeling that well and she is a great admirer of yours. I wonder if you would come over and say hello. We just saw the Kit Cornell show."

"Do you know Kit?" asked the producer, who seemed surprised.

He had a deep voice that seemed to come from a well below the ground.

"No," said Harry, "but I'm a great admirer of hers."

"I see," said the producer, putting on a pair of leather gloves. "I'm afraid I can't stop now, but which one is your mother?"

"The one in the booth," said Harry, pointing toward Glo.

The producer looked over at Harry's mother, smiled, and tipped his hat in her direction. Following his lead, the captain did a little bow that was meant for Glo as well. In response, Glo lifted her water glass and smiled back.

"Thanks," said Harry.

"My pleasure," said the producer, holding out his arm to the captain, who handed him his briefcase. After checking to see that he had all of his possessions, he walked briskly toward the exit on surprisingly short legs.

"What a gracious man," said Glo when Harry slid back into the booth.

"He could have come over."

"Men like that are very busy."

"Maybe I'll be too busy to say hello to his mother someday."

"You never would."

Harry realized he was probably mixing up the producer with Randy. He seemed to be angry at all successful men with trim little mustaches.

"What does he see in her, Glo?"

"I can understand it, Harry."

"Does he know you're sick?"

"I'm fine," said Glo. "I'm with you."

She hooked her arm through his and looked around at the few remaining men who were huddled together in banquettes talking about shows, and the Hirschfield caricatures overhead, and the captain, who did yet another little bow in her direction.

"Harry . . ."

"Yes, Glo."

"Don't you just love this restaurant . . . ?"

Glo remembered an appointment she had made at the corsetiere's and asked if Harry would mind dropping by with her. He was concerned that she might be going in for a fitting, which would mean hours and hours of waiting around, all of which would put a damper on the afternoon. But she assured him that she was only going by to say hello and to let the corsetiere group know that she was still thinking about them, even if she hadn't been in for a while.

When they arrived, Harry took a seat in the reception room and began to leaf through corsetiere magazines while Glo went into the fitting room to see her friends. When he had tired of looking at

pictures of models in corsets and reading about happenings in the
industry, he went downstairs and watched the news as it twirled
around the Times tower on big electric lights. He wondered what
was going to happen to him. It was one thing to see matinees with
Glo and to accompany her to the corsetiere, but Harry wanted more
out of life. When he had watched the same news half a dozen times,
Glo came down, all bubbly and excited, and said she had met the
most wonderful woman in the fitting room, which was why she had
taken so long. The woman was a neighbor whose husband had
prospered as a designer of store-window displays and who had
always seemed stuck-up to Glo.

"But she isn't," said Glo. "She's a wonderful person and she's
anxious to meet you."

"Now?" asked Harry.

"It'll only take a second," said Glo.

She took him by the hand and led him upstairs and into the
fitting room, where a tall woman with white skin and red hair that
she kept tied up in a bun was being fitted for a corset.

"Oh, no," said the woman, falling back and covering her bosom.
"You weren't supposed to bring him in here. You'll embarrass the
boy."

"Oh, stop," said Glo. "He just got out of the Air Force."

"How do you do," said Harry, shaking hands with the woman
and at the same time trying not to look at her. The corset did not
quite cover her backside, and there may have been a tuft of reddish
hair protruding from the front of the garment. Harry felt that it
was worse than being naked.

"I told her about your situation," said Glo, "and she has a
wonderful nephew who is anxious to help you."

"If it's all right with you," said the woman, "I'll call Ben the
minute I get home."

Harry said he appreciated it and that if nobody minded, he
would prefer to wait outside.

"Maybe you're right," said Glo as Harry headed for the fitting-
room door. "Maybe he was a little embarrassed."

"They're all like that," said the woman, trying to get the corset to cover her backside. "My nephew is the same way."

Harry went back to the reception room and tried to stop thinking about the way the woman looked in the corset. He couldn't tell if he was excited by it or not, and decided finally that he probably was.

"Well, you're all set, my darling," said Glo when they were back out on the street.

"I haven't met her nephew yet."

"You're set," said Glo. "Take my word for it. But it's amazing the way I wouldn't speak to that woman for twenty-five years because I thought she had her nose in the air. And she turns out to be the sweetest creature that ever walked the face of the earth.

"It shows you what can happen, Harry, when you occasionally take a nip or two."

~~~ BEN McCARDLE WAS A TALL NEW EN-glander whose manner was an odd combination of tension and relaxation. He sat in his office with his long legs stretched out comfortably before him. But from time to time he would spring to his feet, scratch furiously at his ribs, and peer down the hall as if he were waiting for someone to come and carry him off. From the look of his bulletin board, he appeared to be in charge of a magazine that was no bigger than Harry's wallet. Harry was not entirely sure he wanted to work on that tiny a magazine. It would be like working on no magazine at all. On the other hand, it would be a foot in the door. And it might lead to bigger things.

After reading through Harry's target story, McCardle stroked his chin thoughtfully and said that although it had merit, it could profit from an injection of big themes, such as love, hate, fear, hunger, and sex. Although, strictly speaking, Harry had not been looking for editorial counsel, he thanked McCardle nonetheless and said that he would attempt to work some in.

McCardle said that there was indeed an opening on his staff, but unfortunately he had promised it to a Communist. Harry felt awful about seeing yet another job that was within his grasp slip away. He had liked the homey informal look of the place as he was led into McCardle's office and had been impressed by the rolltop desks that had been assigned to each employee, no matter how lowly. Harry admitted to being disappointed but told McCardle he was not about to take a job away from anyone, even if it was a Communist. Not, he added quickly, that he had any affection for the Bolshevik creed.

"And he's got kids, too," said McCardle unhelpfully.

"That cinches it," said Harry, getting to his feet.

"Easy, easy," said McCardle. "Go easy on Big Ben."

Sliding backward on his swivel chair, he threw up his hands in front of his face, as if someone were about to rain blows down upon him. It was intended to be a charming affectation, but Harry sensed that someone had indeed rained such blows upon him when he was growing up.

"Take a chomp on this sandwich," said McCardle, reaching into a lunch bag. "And let Big Ben sit here and anguish for a while."

He gave the word a French pronunciation so that it came out "sahn-weech."

Though Harry had already eaten, he accepted McCardle's offering, thinking it would be discourteous not to do so. He bit into the sandwich and tasted only relish. Thinking he had made a mistake and missed something, he took a quick peek inside and saw that it was indeed a relish sandwich.

"Good eats," said McCardle. "Courtesy of Mrs. Ben."

Harry said the sandwich was interesting and meant it, although he could not honestly say to the New Englander that he was looking forward to his next one.

McCardle returned to the subject of the Communist job seeker.

"Don't get me wrong. It's not as if the guy isn't opposed to everything that you and I cherish and hold dear. It's just that he has those kids."

"Well, what the hell," he said, winding up a struggle of conscience. "I'll load him up with fwee-lance."

The two men shook hands, Harry wondering about the odd pronunciation of a familiar word.

"Sic transit Communisto Manifesto," said McCardle. "And any fave of Aunt Min's is a fave of mine.

"Incidentally," he said, sliding his chair in close to Harry. "Did you get a glom of her in her corset?"

"Just for a minute," said Harry.

"*Moi aussi,* " said McCardle, popping his eyes.

McCardle filled in Harry on the Wellman Company, which released a great many magazines, the only requirement for each
being that it resemble closely a successful publication put out by
another company. Small bite-size magazines were in vogue at the
moment, the theory behind them being that Americans were on the
move and had little time to settle in with big ones. Several had been
tested successfully by other companies; Wellman felt it was safe
to come in with one of his own, although it was to be watched
closely to see that it had as little character of its own as possible.

"*Allons,*" said McCardle, leaping to his feet. "*Suivez-moi* and
I'll run you past Mr. W."

They caught up with August Wellman in the corridor. He was
a gray-haired man of indeterminate age who wore soft casual
clothing and had the easy manners of a Westerner. At his side was
the busiest man Harry had ever come across. He had his sleeves
rolled up and made notations on charts and memo pads, stopping
to check his watch and then to shake his head as if he had lost
more time than he could afford.

At the approach of McCardle and Harry, Wellman swiveled
around easily, as if he were on a horse, and took a puff of a thin
cigar.

"What is it?"

The question and the deliberate way in which it was asked
caused McCardle to scratch furiously at his neck and ribs. The
busy man speeded up his pace in making notations on a chart.
Pulling himself together, McCardle made a strong case for the
hiring of Harry, saying that it would be a mistake to let him get
away.

"I don't like to make mistakes," said Wellman.

He took another long puff of his cigar, glanced quickly at Harry,
and said: "Give 'em a try."

Then he ambled off, all but kicking the horse that wasn't there.

"Jesus," said McCardle, who gave himself a few more scratches
and then tapered them off.

The busy man introduced himself to Harry as Keith Kaufman.

"I'd like to get to know you," he said, "but I'm just too damned swamped."

He stayed with Harry and McCardle for another ten minutes, anyway, talking about how he was up to his ears in work. Then he excused himself and left, muttering about all the time he had lost.

"What does he do?" asked Harry.

"Beats me," said McCardle. "Wellman met him at his club. I hear he bangs a lot of girls."

McCardle led Harry down the hall to a small cubicle with one of the rolltop desks that Harry had coveted on the way in.

"*Voilà,*" he said. "Your orifice."

Sharing the cubicle with a rolltop desk of her own was a pretty young woman with a large bottom that was in disproportion to her thin spinster's chest. McCardle introduced Harry to the woman, whose name was Miss Portman, and said that henceforth she would serve as Harry's part-time secretary.

"Start by getting him some coffee," said McCardle.

Harry was surprised that McCardle would put his instructions in the form of an almost military command, which he felt was harsh and unnecessary.

When he had left, Harry told Miss Portman that he really didn't need a secretary and that he didn't drink coffee, but her response was to run out of the room crying all the same. Harry felt awful. He had been with the company for only a couple of hours, and already he had cost a Communist his job and sent a young woman flying out of his office in tears. When Miss Portman returned, Harry was not quite sure what to do next, and decided to take up the subject of contemporary literature.

"J. D. Salinger is a great favorite of mine," said Harry, "although there is more to him than meets the eye."

"How can you say that," she said, astonished and near tears again, "when you know perfectly well that it's not true?"

Balling up her fists in anger, she stamped her foot and ran out of the office in tears again. Harry decided that she was the most

153

sensitive person he had ever encountered, and unless he found the key to her complex style, it was going to be difficult to share an office with her.

Later in the day Harry was invited to attend a meeting whose main purpose seemed to be to see to it that several staff members were kept out of it. One was a pale and slender man who could be seen sitting at his desk down the hall and breathing quietly as if he were about to expire. He seemed to have offended McCardle by his strong sense of moral purpose and by generally not being a fun person. The other was a heavyset woman named Tanya, whose high-heeled walk, which was clunky, had driven McCardle to distraction.

"Are they out there?" McCardle asked his secretary, before the meeting began.

"Yes, Big Ben," she said, after a look down the corridor. "I can see him and hear her."

"Good," said McCardle, giving himself a few quick scratches. "See to it that they do not attend this meeting."

The secretary was a thin, short-haired woman who covered an almost constant giggle with one hand and whose body was skewed slightly over to one side so that her skirt was permanently hiked up. Harry had his usual struggle in deciding if this was appealing to him and decided that he wanted her on the spot. Each staff member had a slight physical defect, although there was no evidence they had been chosen for that reason. Still, Harry wondered if his high hips hadn't helped him to edge out the Communist.

Ideas were thrown at McCardle, most of them hard-hitting anti-Communist ones from the managing editor, a wiry man whose hair came down so close to the bridge of his nose that he had virtually no forehead. McCardle received the ideas thoughtfully, giving his assurance that he would chew on them. Not wishing to be left out, Harry, perhaps not thinking it through, suggested a notion about liquor stores that were tragically being held up throughout the nation but received little support for it. He thought he detected a note of backbiting in the air. Surprisingly, considering her genial nature, McCardle's secretary leaned in toward him at one point and said cattily: "I don't recall seeing your name on any mastheads about town."

"Hey, look," said the managing editor, following along with a carping comment of his own, "if Harry wants to write the great American novel, let him go ahead. Let's not stop him. It just doesn't happen to be for the rest of us, that's all."

As the meeting drew to a close, the managing editor threw the subject of his troubled marriage on the table. A difficulty had been that he liked sex in the morning, while his wife preferred to have it after dark, if at all.

"Don't you just love it bright and early?" he asked McCardle's secretary, who giggled characteristically but did not reveal her preference.

As the office emptied out, McCardle asked Harry to stay behind and handed him a packet of Episcopalian sermons with instructions to package them in a breezy manner for the cover of an upcoming issue.

"It's fwee-lance," said McCardle, giving the word the odd pronunciation again and explaining that he would be paid seventy-five dollars for the work, which would be in addition to his salary. McCardle suggested to Harry that he keep this arrangement to himself unless he wanted to report it to the serious man down the hall and torture him.

Harry thanked McCardle and returned to his cubicle, barely able to believe his good fortune. Taking a seat behind his cherished rolltop desk, he heard loud, clumping steps in the hallway and guessed correctly that they signaled the approach of Tanya, whose walk was considered offensive by McCardle. After introducing herself she took up a position behind Harry and began to read over his shoulder, her heavy breasts cushioned against his back as if she were resting them. The sensation was not unpleasant, and Harry allowed her to remain there while he riffled through the sermons.

155

Before the day was over, Harry met the art director, a bearish man with a hearing aid who sat in his office and took on illustrators who had challenged him at arm wrestling. At closing time Harry met him once again in the elevator, which he virtually filled by himself. With a wink the man tapped the packet of sermons beneath Harry's arm and said: "Big Ben give you fwee-lance" thereby clearing up the mystery of the odd pronunciation, which was meant to mock the poor man's speech defect.

Though Harry planned to celebrate his first day of work that night, he saw that there was going to be little time for it and spent the evening instead wrestling with the sermons. He could not make head nor tail out of them, much less figure out a way to make their contents breezy and succinct. Each heavenly thought twinkled briefly before him and went spinning off into nowhere. Thinking he might be going insane, he asked Glo for some help. But after borrowing a neighbor's glasses and reading them over several times, she handed them back.

"I'd like to help you, Harry," she said, reverting to her old lusty style, "but I can't understand a goddamned word of this."

Sleepless and frustrated, Harry returned to McCardle's office the next morning, prepared to hand in his resignation.

"I just can't cut it," said Harry, feeling miserable.

McCardle seemed unfazed by this development. As he returned the sermons to their file cabinet, he explained that they had been written by his father and that Harry was not the first to grapple unsuccessfully with them.

"There's a hundred bucks in it for the old geezer if I can just get someone to package them.

"But no *tragadero,*" he added. "Win some, lose some. It's the kind of thing that binds us together in this great nation of ours."

McCardle suggested that Harry try a subject that might have more tang to it—the connection between sex and cigarette smoking. Properly researched, he felt it would attract a large audience. Sensing a second disaster, Harry returned to his cubicle in a panic that subsided when he thought of his old friend Appleman, who might be just the man to provide the proper scholarly underpinning. With some trepidation he asked the outrageously sensitive Miss Portman if she would mind monitoring a call to Appleman, which would put Harry more at his ease in throwing out questions to his old friend. To his surprise she accepted with something approaching cheerfulness.

Harry called Appleman, who got Harry off to a running start by tossing off a few notions that tied cigarette smoking in with sexuality in general, and the phallus in particular. Sheepishly Appleman confessed that he had not made the penis a principal area of concentration but gave Harry the names and numbers of colleagues who had. When Harry hung up, he noticed that Miss Portman's eyes had become misty but that in this case her tears were happy ones.

"Who was that?" she asked.

"Bob Appleman," said Harry. "The most interesting man I know."

"He certainly is," said Miss Portman. "I'd give anything to meet him."

Harry said that he did not think such a meeting would be difficult to arrange and called Appleman back to report that his secretary had listened in on their conversation and was anxious to get together with him. Snuffling into the phone in his disarming way, Appleman said he would be delighted to take her to dinner sometime. After telling Miss Portman the good news, Harry spent the rest of the morning talking to Appleman's colleagues, each of whom was only too happy to draw up an increasingly airtight connection between cigarette smoking and penises.

At lunchtime Harry accompanied McCardle to a weekly buying session that was held in the large, baronial cellar of a popular German restaurant. They were soon joined by a dozen middle-aged men, each of whom wore a badly fitted overcoat and carried a bulging suitcase. When the men had made themselves comfort-

able, they gathered around a buffet table along with Harry and
McCardle and began to lift toasts to the tall New Englander and
his family, and to present him with gifts such as cuff links and
ornate Bavarian drinking mugs. When it was discovered that two
of the men had given McCardle identical neckties, one of them was
tossed over to Harry.

The group then adjourned to a large round table for a satisfying
lunch of wiener schnitzel à la Holstein and dumplings; afterward
the men took turns passing along sets of photographs to McCardle,
most of which featured the activities of sword swallowers and
female contortionists. From what Harry was able to gather, the
salesmen, Central European, for the most part, had smuggled the
photographs across the border in their flight from Nazi Germany.
As McCardle stroked his chin and made his selections, the men
exchanged comments on his discerning eye.

"Amazing," said one to a colleague when McCardle had re-
versed the order of a set of photographs, "the way he takes something banal and gives it just the right little twist."

He illustrated this by doing a little twist in the air with one hand.

Harry wondered why McCardle would want to purchase quite so
many contortionist pictures, but he respected his friend's judgment
enormously and guessed that he had tapped into some hidden vein
of reader interest.

As the purchasing session continued, Harry became increasingly aware of one salesman in particular, who sat unaggressively
at the far end of the table and seemed familiar-looking. Suddenly
he realized that it was his old friend Schmuel, with whom he had
driven cross-country after his discharge from the Air Force.
Amazingly he had turned up as a seller of female contortionist
pictures.

Toward the end of the lunch, as brandies and cigars were being
passed around, Harry moved across to him and told him what a
treat it was to see him again.

"Then how come you don't buy any of these pictures," said

Schmuel with a shrug, pulling a few of the rejected ones out of his suitcase.

Harry explained that he had just joined the company and was not in a buying position.

"So tell your friend," said Schmuel, holding up several of the rejects for Harry's inspection. "These are beautiful pictures. The best."

Harry said that at the next scheduled lunch, when he was on a firmer footing, he would press McCardle to consider Schmuel's selections more carefully.

"Who said I'm coming to the next lunch?" said Schmuel. "You think I need your help? I piss on you and I piss on your organization.

"Beautiful pictures like this," he muttered, walking off. "And they don't buy one of them."

Harry was disappointed by Schmuel's attitude but gratified that he had at least come out of his shell and found a voice.

"What's with the twerp?" said McCardle, coming over with a brandy snifter. "Want me to pop him one?"

"He's all right," said Harry. "I knew him in the Air Force. His entire family was wiped out in the camps."

"Gleeks," said McCardle, wincing. "Maybe I should have bought his pix."

One of the Europeans approached and stretched high to put his arm around the tall New Englander.

"You know what I like about Big Ben?" he asked.

"What's that" asked Harry.

"You can put a bunch of absolute shit in front of him, and inevitably he picks out ze vun diamond."

Harry called Sally that night to tell her about his tryout at the Wellman Company. Sally said that coincidentally, she, too, had been given a tryout as an instructor in posture at a local charm school. The arrangement was that for each girlfriend of hers she recruited for the school, she would be given a week of free posture instruction for herself. Harry instantly saw that this was horribly unfair and wanted to get his hands on the shyster who had talked her into it.

"I'd fly out there immediately," he said, "if I wasn't having this tryout."

It confirmed his feelings that Sally needed to be protected and that God only knew what would happen to her if he were to break off their engagement.

Sally asked Harry if there were any opportunities in posture in the East. Harry said that he did not know of any at the moment but that he would look into the matter immediately. In the meanwhile the best course would be for her to sit tight while he saw his tryout through and they would take it from there.

〰〰 HARRY WAS IN McCARDLE'S OFFICE THE following day when Appleman and Miss Portman turned up, hand in hand, to announce that they were getting married and that she would be leaving the company immediately.

This took Harry by surprise and McCardle as well.

"Hmm," he said, stroking his chin in a grave manner. "This decision gives Big Ben cause for concern about his team."

He acknowledged, however, that marriage was a good thing, not only for the happy couple but also for the nation at large. Graciously, Harry felt, considering the short notice Miss Portman had given him, he offered to put together a cocktail party for the couple that very evening. Miss Portman and Appleman accepted with eagerness.

"Excellenzo," said McCardle. "I'll call Mrs. Ben and tell the little rascal not to wait up."

The party was held in an editorial bullpen beside McCardle's office. It began conservatively with Appleman, who was strangely awkward in social situations, being introduced stiffly to the Wellman team. The serious man who had been excluded from all meetings put in a rare appearance, as did the cheerful and bosomy Tanya. The simian-looking managing editor entertained the group mildly with an accurate imitation of Senator Joe McCarthy berating a reluctant witness with the words "Don't be cute." In what had become a silent ritual, Tanya took up a position behind Harry and listened attentively with her breasts propped up comfortably against his shoulders.

McCardle picked up the pace by beginning to holler out outra-

161

geous puns that alluded to the future bridegroom's chosen profession.

"*Ego* his way," he said, pointing to Appleman, "and I go mine."

Then, snatching up his secretary, he danced cheek to cheek with her around the room, singing "*Id* Had to Be You."

Appleman acknowledged each of the puns with a shy snuffle into a nonalcoholic drink.

When a calm threatened to settle over the room, McCardle went a step further by flinging his giggling secretary up in the air, causing her skirt to hike up and thrillingly expose a pair of pink panties. Scratching his chest in imitation of primitive man, the bearish art director lumbered forward, carried her off to his office, and did not return immediately.

Harry felt oddly disconnected. He tried to wedge himself into a conversation between two women from accounting who were discussing bowel regularity but was unable to do so with enthusiasm. Feeling a need to help along with the merrymaking, Harry, who was not good at jokes, told one all the same that he had heard in the Air Force to a group that included the serious man. It dealt with an elderly black man being asked what he thought of the impending marriage of a racially mixed couple.

"As long as they loves each other" was the punch line, delivered in dialect.

The serious man balled up his fists in anger and fixed Harry with a look that indicated he saw nothing funny in the story. Harry realized instantly that he was absolutely right and that he had made a horrible blunder. He was stunned by his own insensitivity and barely noticed it when August Wellman showed up along with Keith Kaufman, his constantly busy associate.

"What's going on?" he asked.

"It's a cocktail party," said McCardle, pointing at Appleman and Miss Portman, "for these two crazy kids who've decided to take the plunge."

"Who's paying for it?" he asked.

McCardle drew himself up with dignity.

THE CURRENT CLIMATE

"Big Ben is footing the bill."

"He's giving himself fwee-lance," said the art director, laughing nervously at his remark and looking around for approval.

Wellman took an unusually long puff of his cigar and studied the white ash at the end of it.

"See to it that the book ships on time," he said finally.

Keith Kaufman followed the publisher down the hall, stopping to turn and wink at the group and to pat the air with both hands, as if to indicate that if there were any difficulties, he would see to it that Wellman was assuaged. But the visit had caused McCardle to scratch furiously at his neck and ribs, and the art director to make elaborate adjustments to his hearing aid.

Harry continued to feel humiliated and began to drink heavily. He became angry at Appleman, who stood at the side of his bride-to-be with what came across to Harry as smugness. Though Harry could not imagine that he was being jealous, he wondered if he had missed something in the unspectacular Miss Portman, who stood beaming at Appleman's side, and who seemed, overnight, to have become free of neurosis.

In a pose he had always wanted to imitate, Harry took up a position in the center of the room and, with his legs rakishly set apart, began to drink directly from a bottle. After several long pulls he began to berate his friend Appleman for having abandoned him and for not having been in touch once since their turtle dinner.

Appleman received the attack with lowered head and the quiet dignity that was certain to send him a long way in his chosen profession.

"I'm sorry, Harry," he said with a snuffle. "But it was either you or the woman I've come to love."

Appleman's sudden announcement of his marriage to Miss Portman only served to underscore Harry's feelings of loneliness. He was tempted to call Sally and ask her to come East immediately but decided instead to lose himself in his work at the Wellman Company. He got the hang of it quickly and was chosen by McCar-

163

dle to head up the popular Scratch the Surface series in which each month, an American city, known for its rectitude, was shown to be hypocritical. All one had to do was "scratch the surface" to see that it was a sin pit. Harry did well at this and within weeks was being congratulated for the new energy he had brought to the ailing How'd Ya Like Ta feature, in which a photograph of a pretty woman in a bathing suit was shown, along with a caption that lip-smackingly asked the reader how he would like, if she were a farm girl, to peel her onions, or, in the case of a bank employee, to juggle her assets. Harry did less well with the popular Personal Disaster series in which travelers who had suffered awful bites in the tropics and handymen who had been flung onto high-tension wires recounted their grisly stories. When readership fell off under his direction, the feature was turned back to the simian-looking managing editor, who clucked his tongue at what he saw as Harry's artistic leanings.

At Christmas, Harry was delighted to learn, however, that he was one of the Wellman employees who had been singled out for a bonus. Straining a bit for a Gallic twist, McCardle described it as a "beau-new." Harry continued to admire his tall New England mentor and strove to emulate him by sitting in hard-backed chairs and eating cucumber sandwiches. He became prouder than ever of their association when an Appleman colleague stormed in one day to confront Harry and protest the use of his comments linking cigarette smoking to penises.

Harry recognized him as being the handsome older man with whom Appleman had struck up a conversation over turtle steaks at the fish restaurant.

"I had no idea," he said, slamming his fist down on Harry's desk, "that I would be quoted in a magazine of this kind."

"What kind is that?" said McCardle, appearing suddenly and rising up almost biblically above the man.

"It's hard to say," said the man, retreating immediately and lighting up a cigarette. "Different, I suppose, from what I had imagined."

THE CURRENT CLIMATE

Before the morning was over, the man had signed on to do a column of sex tips.

In his free moments Harry enjoyed poking his head into other departments, such as sports and the bustling little paperback group. He became fascinated by a tall, spirited man who sat in the tiniest cubicle of all, which was beside a broom closet; his head scraped the ceiling and there was barely enough room for his legs. It was pointed out to Harry that he had once been at the head of the company's largest division, with a sea of assistants stretching out before him, but that the market for his comedic magazines had suddenly disappeared. Unwilling to face letting him go, the erratically generous Wellman had reduced his operation drastically in the hope that he would quit in humiliation. But the man refused to do so and chose instead to work happily on, convinced his empire would return. Harry admired his spirit and from time to time would peer in at him in his tiny office and ask how he was getting along.

"Just great," said the man, working confidently away with scissors and paste pot, as if he were in exactly the position he wanted to be.

Also intriguing to Harry was the fan section, in which every inch of the walls was covered by pinned-up glossy photographs of film stars. On a whim he approached its gruff and chain-smoking director on behalf of Glo and was delighted to be given a packet of Barbara Stanwyck pictures for his mother to organize on a freelance basis.

"No need to thank me," said the woman when Harry tried to do so. "Just hand them to mom and go about your business."

With barely a look at Harry, she continued to pound away at her Underwood typewriter, in continuance of some gruff pulp tradition.

Overall, Harry enjoyed his work tremendously and felt that he had pulled off a robbery each time he was given his paycheck. But though his days were lively, Harry's social life continued to be negligible. He enjoyed his brief contacts with the cheerful and large-bodied Tanya, who showed up from time to time to read

165

unsolicited manuscripts over his shoulder, after first depositing her breasts against him. One day he wheeled around and asked her out for a drink. They kissed furiously at a nearby tavern, Tanya indicating her willingness to go to a hotel with him. They then began an odyssey on foot throughout the city, stopping to kiss hungrily beneath awnings and in alleyways. Yet each time they entered a hotel lobby, Harry became flustered and confused as to how actually to register for a room. After hours of this he finally threw up his hands and saw the puzzled but still good-natured Tanya off in a cab.

Harry was invited regularly to his friend Travis's apartment, and would take along with him as a dinner gift a packet of photographs of rural beauties. As rejects, they did not have to meet publication standards; the result was that an occasional nipple was revealed and, in a rare case, magically, a strand or two of pubic hair. Harry presented them to his friend in an affectionate and prearranged ritual.

"Here are your dirties," he would say with a click of his heels, as if they were diplomatic papers.

"Thank you very much, Herr Towns," Travis would respond.

After a little bow he would turn smartly on his heels and whisk them off to his gloomy bedroom. A dark and hauntingly beautiful widow, who worked in a neighborhood diner, had somehow attached herself to the household, cooking chicken dinners for Travis and his look-alike mother, whose eyes and teeth shone like jewelry. It was clear that she was fond of Travis and would happily have moved in with him, perhaps giving her child a decent upbringing, but Travis's mind remained fastened on the series of blond and rural farm girls who had rejected him in Idaho. After dinner Travis, using his fist to simulate a microphone, would spin around the room, singing popular ballads that dealt with heartbreak and lost love. As a sign-off to the evenings, he would drop to his knees and lead cheers for the inhabitants of a ghostly stadium.

* * *

THE CURRENT CLIMATE

One night Randy called and asked Harry to meet him at a large and drafty cafeteria beneath an elevated train. Silently the two men ate fruit salads and, in a tradition of theirs, shared an order of cherry cheesecake. Harry had the feeling that Randy, who looked haggard, wanted to ask him about Glo but could not bring himself to do so. Still, it was a communion of sorts, and when they hugged and said good-bye, Harry got to feel his father's rough beard.

~~~ SALLY ARRIVED IN MANHATTAN SEV-
eral weeks later, along with her parents and several
dozen of her relatives. She called Harry, who came over
to her hotel to meet her during his lunch hour. The
relatives milled about the lobby aimlessly and seemed to
have no organized plan of activity. When Harry wondered about them, Sally said they had decided to come East as a
bloc to see musicals. She took some time coming into focus, but
once she did, Harry saw that Sally was every bit as beautiful as
she had been when he had picked her out of the rubble, following
the collision of the Chevy with her streetcar. She looked at him—
as she had before—in a puzzled way, as if she had expected him
to be someone else and was faintly disappointed. After an embrace
that was both passionate and casual, they took seats in the lobby
and were awkward with each other as always.

Harry asked her if she recalled a favorite restaurant of theirs,
which was owned by a radio announcer.

"Yes," said Sally.

"So do I," said Harry. "Wasn't the steak great?"

"I know," said Sally.

"And the salad?"

"That was good too."

They sat together glumly, neither able to come up with choice
topics for further conversation. After several minutes of this Sally
said her parents were out of the hotel at the moment; if Harry cared
to, they could go upstairs and sit in the room. Harry agreed to do
so. They made love once they were alone, with Harry bringing into
play some of the techniques that he had added to his repertoire

168

since he had last seen her. Sally seemed puzzled by all of this and complained of feeling uncomfortable. Harry was disappointed, although, oddly, he was relieved as well.

After dressing in silence they returned to the lobby, joining Sally's relatives, who seemed bored and had begun to snap at one another. With some sadness Sally and Harry agreed that since it had not gone well in the hotel room and they had been apart so long, there didn't seem to be much reason for them to continue seeing each other. They kissed then with more warmth than they ever had before. Harry shook hands with Sally and started for the door, but the thought of losing her and never again getting to smell her hair was nauseating, so he turned around and suggested they get married, after all.

"Do you think we should?" asked Sally.

"Oh, well," said Harry, in a try for charm. "What the hay."

Arrangements were easily struck in the lobby, with members of Sally's family springing into action and making calls to caterers. Sally's parents arrived soon afterward. Mrs. Turner continued to look at Harry warily, but Mr. Turner easily compensated for his wife's coolness by insisting on giving him his watch. Using the lobby phone, Harry got in touch with Glo, who seemed to have been waiting resignedly for his call and offered to pay for the flowers and the band. Harry then called his father and got Trudy instead, who suggested that they get a famous rabbi who was a friend of hers to preside.

Later in the day Harry escorted Sally to his office and proudly presented her to McCardle, who stood up gallantly to kiss her hand. Taking Harry aside, he said, "She's quite a looker."

As it happened, McCardle's wife was coming in to meet him for dinner that night, and arrangements were made for the two couples to have dinner at a supper club. Mrs. McCardle was a mere slip of a thing who kept her head lowered throughout the meal. At its conclusion McCardle said: "Mrs. Ben is eager to dance with you, fella, but she is too shy to ask." Harry said it was fine with him

169

and led her to the dance floor. She clung to him damply, her body trembling as if they were concluding a long and melancholy affair. Sally danced with McCardle but soon began to whirl about on her own, doing wild flamenco steps, her fingers snapping sharply overhead. At the end of the evening McCardle took his wife off to the country, and Harry drove Sally back to her hotel, the two kissing perfunctorily in the lobby and agreeing that it had been a fine evening.

The following day McCardle asked Harry into his office and said that he and Mrs. McCardle, after some thought, had concluded that Harry should not go ahead with the marriage.

"Why's that, Big Ben?" asked Harry.

"Ah, jeez, fella," said McCardle, suddenly awkward, "she's got a lot of problems."

Harry was outraged at the suggestion and could not help but think that it related to Mrs. McCardle's interest in him. Needless to say, it made him more determined than ever to press on with his plans.

Trudy arranged for the couple to be interviewed on the weekend in the oak-lined midtown chambers of the celebrated Rabbi Ross, whom she felt would be a good candidate to officiate at their wedding. A tall and troubled-looking man, the rabbi served as unofficial spokesman for a wealthy section of the Jewish community and was not reluctant to comment on world affairs. Harry had read a capsule summary of one of his speeches, in which he declared his opposition to war but agreed that from time to time it could not be avoided. Harry and Sally took seats in Rabbi Ross's study, joining other couples who were awaiting their interviews. After they had been seen by the rabbi the couples would emerge from his chambers, smiling exultantly. The rabbi, his arms around them, would show them benevolently to the door. When it was the turn of Harry and Sally and they were seated in his chambers, the rabbi said that he had agreed to see them because of his long association with Trudy, who had advised him on money management.

"What are your occupations?" he asked.

Harry said he was the associate editor of a bite-size magazine that was put out by the Wellman Company and that Sally was in posture. After taking a moment to digest this information the rabbi walked to the window and began to drum his fingers on the sill.

"I'll have to mull it over," he said finally.

Convinced that they had done poorly, Harry and Sally were surprised when later in the day they received a call from the rabbi, who said he would agree to officiate but only on condition that he be paid in cash before the ceremony.

Until the last moment Harry half expected someone to materialize and take him aside and tell him to come to his senses. Only McCardle had made such an effort, and Harry mistrusted his intentions, feeling that he had been influenced by his love-starved wife. Therefore he felt that he had no choice but to plunge ahead. For his best man he decided on Travis, who not only turned him down flatly but did so with irritation, as if he thought Harry was insane to ask him to do such a thing. Harry next called his friend Dandy Boisseau, who accepted and immediately shipped off a huge oil painting of a blues singer as a wedding gift.

The ceremony was held in a hotel that was a favorite of athletic teams that competed in a nearby stadium. Harry was familiar with its restaurant, which was mediocre but served excellent dinner rolls. After an unhappy summer romance Harry had been unable to eat for several weeks, his appetite returning only when he was taken by Glo to the hotel restaurant. He had always felt it was the rolls that had brought him around.

Sally was radiant in her bridal gown, although, disappointingly, her hair had been swept back severely in the style of a Spanish dancer. A wedding ring somehow materialized and was passed along from Turner to Turner until it reached Harry, who ceremoniously slipped it on Sally's finger. Though Harry felt that Rabbi

171

BRUCE JAY FRIEDMAN

Ross's officiation was mechanical, he enjoyed leaping up in the air and smashing the ritual glass. The band struck up a chorus of "Anniversary Song," with Harry and Sally the first to take the floor to a smattering of applause. As a dancer, Harry had never mastered the technique of reversing his steps. The result was that he was restricted to traveling as far in one direction as he was able to, and then walking his partner back to their starting point so that they could begin again. After several rounds of this Sally suggested that they mingle with the other guests.

Harry joined Dandy Boisseau, who had been circulating among the puzzled Turners, telling them that the bridegroom was known to have strengthened race relations. Harry assured the Turners that this was an exaggeration. Mr. Turner was as good-natured as ever, handing Harry a series of gifts and finally taking him downstairs and giving him his Buick. When they returned, Mr. Turner unaccountably began to circle Randy, patting him on the head and saying, "You baldies are the greatest." Randy, who had come to the wedding alone, seemed bewildered and unable to respond. Though his hair had receded a bit, he barely qualified as a skinhead. Harry took his part, suggesting that Mr. Turner had been insensitive and threatening to return the Buick. Sally stepped between the two men and led off her father, returning to apologize to Randy and to suggest that Mr. Turner had never been the same since he had begun to sell fumigants.

"I wish you could have known him years ago," she said, speaking at greater length than was her custom. "He was so handsome. He would take me in his arms and I would smell his chest. You should have smelled that man's chest."

Randy seemed touched by the remarks and led Sally off to dance, possibly so that she could smell *his* chest. When Harry next saw Randy, he was kneeling gallantly beside Glo, as if he were courting her. Harry felt that if his mother and father were to get back together, his marriage at least would have served a useful purpose.

An arrangement had been made for Harry and Sally to stay at

172

the hotel for several nights and then go off on a brief honeymoon. Both families had combined resources to rent a small apartment for them in midtown Manhattan. Immediately after the wedding, Harry found that he was furiously hungry and went downstairs to the restaurant to see if he could eat some of the rolls he had loved as a boy. The management was reluctant to give them to anyone who was not a dinner guest, but relented when Harry called upstairs and was able to prove that he was a newlywed.

After wolfing down several of the rolls, Harry joined Sally in the hotel room.

"Looks like we're married now," he said.

"It sure does," said Sally.

When they had undressed and gotten into bed, a siren sounded in the distance. Sally wondered about it.

Harry guessed that it might be a relic of World War Two. Not all of them had been gathered up, and from time to time, one went off of its own accord.

"You know so much," said Sally, "and I don't know anything."

"You know a lot," said Harry.

Then he entered her from another angle, and she found the result tolerable. Afterward they clung to each other and thus began their marriage.

Harry and Sally traveled to Florida on their honeymoon, stopping at a resort hotel that catered to newlywed couples from the South. Their marriages seemed shaky from the start, with plump brides in particular flirting openly with the husbands of their girlfriends in the elevator. Harry himself fell madly in love with a woman in the pool area but decided it would be a nuisance to follow her to the Carolinas. Upon their return they moved into a narrow space in a Manhattan town house that had once been a section of a palatial apartment. Though modest in size, it remained grand in its marbled look. Immediately upon settling in, they received a visit from Sally's friend Tammy, the one who had one breast larger than the other. She found fault with the apartment

173

and its lack of modern conveniences, making Sally restless in it from the start. Harry paid little attention to Tammy, since he recalled that she had allowed a boyfriend who was a salesman to pee on her leg regularly.

They forged ahead with the marriage, Harry returning to his job while Sally canvassed the city in search of opportunities in posture.

No sooner had Harry returned than a series of calamities struck the Wellman Company. In Harry's absence Keith Kaufman had slipped off treacherously, along with the simianlike managing editor, to begin a chain of magazines that would be imitative of the Wellman publications, which were, of course, imitations of others. Though all signs pointed to a quick failure, Wellman's feelings of betrayal were strong. An added setback was the disappearance, almost overnight, of reader interest in bite-size magazines. Wellman's thoughts turned to economy, and he asked that McCardle's bulging inventory be brought before him.

Soon afterward McCardle reported to the office of the publisher at the head of a column of staff members, each of whom had been instructed to carry in an armload of the suspect files. Wellman was shocked at what he saw and could only wonder why McCardle would want to invest hundreds of thousands of dollars of the firm's money in contortionist pictures. With McCardle standing by and wincing at each of the blows, Wellman smacked each set of the offending photographs.

When the bloodletting had ended, Harry accompanied McCardle to his office. All things considered, he felt that the New Englander had behaved with dignity. But once he reached his own quarters, McCardle collapsed in his swivel chair, his long legs stretched out before him.

"Can you believe it?" he said, his head in his hands. "He smacked Big Ben's entire inventory."

The following day, Harry was summoned to appear in Wellman's office. There he found the publisher in his characteristic stance, staring out at the city and puffing on a thin cigar. Without preamble,

THE CURRENT CLIMATE

Wellman said that he had been thinking of starting up a new magazine that would combine the upscale features of *The New Yorker* and *Esquire,* yet have a flavor of its own, which would be kept to a minimum. Sex would be represented in the form of photographs and a sprinkling of hot words such as *dark triangle.* If lagging sales caused more sex than that to be needed, Wellman's name was to be removed from the masthead so that he would not be mocked in his community. The editor's name would replace his and be displayed in larger type. It was Wellman's intention to use excellent paper in a front section and to work in more of it as the publication caught on. The title he had chosen was *Classy.* He had been after it for years and was pleased that it had become available.

"Do you think you can handle it?"

Harry's first thought was to the effect this would have on McCardle, who had been his friend and mentor. Clearly, though, the publisher had thought this through and had been unforgiving of the New Englander for investing a fortune of the company's money in contortionist pictures. Harry had little idea of why he had been chosen for this important job and was troubled by the title, although he had to concede that it was straightforward. He decided to accept. Wellman said he felt he had made a good decision and that he would see about a rise in the near future. Harry wondered if this was the same as a raise but felt it would be impolite to ask. Wellman said that Harry would have as his secretary the cheerful man in the tiny cubicle who had once headed up a staff of hundreds. No doubt he felt that this ultimate humiliation would cause him finally to leave the firm.

Harry was given access to Wellman's cigar box and told that he could use the bathroom when it was not occupied by his nephew, who visited occasionally and spent a great deal of time in there.

Harry went immediately to see McCardle and caught him emptying out his desk and preparing to leave the company. Seeing his friend in this condition, Harry felt he had no choice but to offer to leave with him, which he did lamely. McCardle graciously assured him it wasn't necessary.

175

"It's time for Big Ben to hit the trail, anyway."

He congratulated Harry, telling him hats off and not to feel bad about the way things had worked out. Harry knew the rest of the litany. It was the American way. The kind of thing we had fought and died for. Wasn't this what tied us together? In this great nation of ours? The patriotic spoofing had less edge to it than usual. The loss of his job was a terrible blow to McCardle. And it wasn't true that Harry had done nothing to advance his own situation. Whenever Wellman was in the area, he had made it a point to hunch forward in his chair, as if he were seething with ideas. For all he knew, the tactic may have put him over the top.

Though the victory had a sad note to it, Harry and Sally decided to celebrate all the same. In anticipation of either a rise or a raise, they bought wrought-iron sconces and a department-store print of Raoul Dufy, whose work was in vogue. They had dinner at a neighborhood Italian restaurant and were delighted to find that a child star was one of the customers and had ordered the same clam dish as they had. Later they took an aimless walk along Fifth Avenue, with Sally remarking idly that she would not mind cocking out a few babies. Though Harry flinched at the unlovely words and hoped they were intended to be satirical, he took note of this feeling of hers. For the moment, though, he felt it had nothing to do with him. Holding hands, they returned home and watched a television game-show hostess kiss her dinner companion timidly on the lips in the doorway of her brownstone. Though the man was not her husband, they could not decide if they had seen something scandalous. All in all, it was a pleasant if not overly romantic evening.

Although Harry was grateful for the opportunity to head up a magazine that was slavishly imitative of existing ones, it was Wellman's dream, not his. After several days of the new function Harry perversely returned to his old Korean target story, ever more determined to whip it into an appealing form. With his nights thus occupied, Sally was forced to spend a great deal of time on her own and began to see more of two new friends: a rudderless blond girl she had met in a department store; and her husband, who sold insurance. One night Sally returned late and told Harry that her new friend had admitted to sleeping with any man who asked her to, and that her husband had homosexual affairs in train stations. Harry was madly aroused by this disclosure and wanted to pounce on Sally's new friend at once. Since this was unworkable, he fell upon Sally, who wondered what had come over him.

Soon afterward Harry was visited by two members of the Wellman business staff who presented him with a plan to launch the first issue of *Classy* with ten pages of truss ads. Harry felt this would throw off the tone irreparably and refused to go along with it. The two men, who obviously derived healthy commissions from the truss industry, kept after Harry, giving him good-natured pokes in the ribs and inviting him to their office to watch a pornographic film. Though Harry had never seen one and was tempted to take a peek, he decided it would compromise his position so he turned down the offer. All three marched grimly into the office of Wellman, who heard arguments from both parties and ended up cutting the number of truss pages back to six. When Harry insisted than even six such pages would send the wrong signal to prospective readers, Mr. Wellman took a puff of his thin cigar and said he had put through a rise.

Though Harry continued to be irritated by the offensive ad campaign, he nonetheless proceeded to put together the debut edition of *Classy*. Approaching famed authors with trepidation, he was surprised at how many were willing to release their work to a fledgling publication. One of Harry's favorite authors, who constructed hard-boiled yet sophisticated detective fiction, invited Harry to have a drink with him in a basement apartment he had rented in a West Side brownstone. Harry found him to be attractively down-to-earth in the style of his detective heroes, and as handsome as a movie star. After sending a Chinese man out for a bottle of bourbon, he told Harry that he had just returned from

177

Hollywood, where he had settled up matters relating to his fourth divorce. He proposed that he write a new story especially designed for the debut issue of *Classy,* his only condition being that he be paid for it as quickly as possible. Harry could not believe his good fortune. Without thinking through the ramifications, he longed to be living in a basement apartment, sending a Chinese man out for whiskey and settling up matters relating to his fourth divorce.

As a counterbalance to the offending truss ads, Harry thought he might try to bring some cachet to the pinup department. Casting about for fresh new talent, he was advised that the classiest of all newcomers was a man named Peter Smalley. Harry wangled an appointment with the rising young star, who turned out to be none other than his old friend Schmuel in yet another incarnation. In the months since Harry had last seen him as an agent for contortionist pictures, he had Anglicized his name and taken on effete airs. Greeting Harry at the door of his handsomely appointed studio, he wore a silk dressing gown and smoked a gold-tipped Russian cigarette.

"Come in, come in, old boy," he said, steering Harry past a bank of receptionists. "I shan't be a second."

The Israeli disappeared and then returned, holding a single photograph at the edges with two fingers, as if it were a rare butterfly specimen. After placing it delicately before Harry, he leapt back, held his hands behind his head, and clapped them smartly, as if he were signaling to a tango partner. The subject was a popular model posing coyly in a nightgown. Harry had seen better photographs of her although none so dimly lighted. He wondered if he could see another. With some annoyance the Israeli danced forth with a companion photograph but said that two was all that Harry could expect to be shown. In spite of himself, Harry felt the pressure of the Israeli's fame and allowed himself to be bullied into buying the murky photographs for astronomical prices. He regretted this decision instantly in the corridor.

Soon afterward Harry received a call from a man named Rene Steinman, who said he had met Harry in Carl Boisseau's writing course. The voice sounded familiar; Harry wondered if he could possibly be the same man whose harsh criticism had caused him to flee and not to return.

"Didn't you say my work was sick?" asked Harry.

"I did say that," Steinman conceded, "and I'm sure it hurt you. I'm sure it hurt a lot. But the piece has continued to nag at me. I've since given up my own writing—I'm a theater director now—and it suddenly occurred to me what was wrong. It needs to be done on the stage. In the theater it wouldn't have to be sick at all. Not one bit. And that's why I'm calling. To ask you to consider letting me help you turn your wonderful target-range piece into a play."

Though Steinman's old attack still rankled, Harry felt it took some character on his part to make the call. And the invitation was flattering; Harry agreed to meet the director that very night at a famed dairy restaurant on the Lower East Side.

Harry liked the beret-wearing Steinman at this meeting, proving that first encounters, however disastrous, can be misleading. Since his switch to the theater, Steinman had taken on an earthy, prole-tariat style, scratching his belly openly, using toothpicks, and allowing his stomach to hang sloppily over his belt. After a moment or two of stiffness the two men ordered dinner and set about discussing how to convert Harry's Korean target story into a piece for the theater, an area in which Steinman had become knowledge-able. This was the first of many such sessions. By day Harry pushed ahead with *Classy;* by night he met Steinman in dairy restaurants for further collaboration. The heavy load produced a further strain on Harry's marriage, though it was barely notice-able, since Sally was asleep by the time Harry had wrapped up his work at the restaurant and returned home late at night.

Wellman tested the first issue of *Classy* in his usual manner by placing a pile of them at his favorite newsstand and then standing in the shadow to observe the rate at which people snapped them up. After several such tests he appeared in Harry's office one morning and smacked a copy lightly, indicating that it was moving, although not briskly. Nonetheless he authorized a second edition and assigned his nephew to Harry's staff.

In the meantime Steinman had drummed up interest in Harry's play on the part of a producer who agreed to mount a small production on the condition that a scene involving the Seminoles be strengthened. Harry was enormously excited by this news. Though he and Sally had discussed a vacation trip, he broke off all talk about this and rushed off to meet Steinman that night at their favorite dairy restaurant. Untypically the two allowed themselves a cocktail to celebrate their success and then set about to repair the weak section.

Sally appeared soon after and was either enormously light-hearted or drunk. In an uncharacteristic show of affection, she sat on Harry's lap and threw her arms around him. The target of this activity seemed to be Steinman, who reacted by crossing his legs and snapping open a copy of a left-wing journal. Sally said that she had bought two tickets for a vacation on a cruise ship and hoped that Harry would come along. Harry looked first at the noncommittal Steinman and then at Sally. He left the restaurant with his wife.

〜〜 THE SYMBOLISM WAS NOT LOST ON Harry. Nonetheless he did his best to crank up his spirits and to set about enjoying himself with Sally. They had always been at their best on vacations.

The ship was a converted freighter that had seen extensive wartime service and was in dilapidated condition. To give it a festive air, the management had hung lanterns and party banners around the deck. To some extent it worked. The accumulated strain of Harry's two careers dropped away as the boat sailed farther out to sea. Sally, who had run into a brick wall in her search for work in the field of posture, became increasingly gay as well. She did her spirited exhibitionist dancing on deck. Instead of merely observing, Harry joined in, matching her whirl for whirl with only occasional corrections from Sally on his style. It seemed to Harry that she was hopelessly beautiful; he was sickeningly in love with her.

On their third night at sea, word came to them in their cabin that the captain wished them to be his guests at dinner. They accepted and were curious as to what it would be like.

The captain was a stiff and fiery-eyed Cypriot who gave off an impression of enormous physical power. Harry and Sally were happy to see that the food was tasty, in sharp comparison to their previous meals, which had barely been edible. Throughout the dinner the captain conversed with several world-traveling British couples and rarely looked in their direction. This convinced Harry that they were at the center of his attention. Toward the end of the meal the captain began to make philosophical observations, most of them concerning the sea and to the effect that it was wise and all-knowing. Gradually he turned toward Harry, who felt somehow that he was being challenged. Though he was embarrassed by wisdoms, Harry found himself saying that all men had the same dreams. This seemed to upset the captain.

"I don't understand," he said. "Do you mean I have the same dreams as the cabin boy?"

"Yes," said Harry.

"And the cook?" said the captain, changing color.

"The very same."

The captain took hold of the table as if to steady himself. Gradually he got control of himself and turned to Sally.

"Your husband plays the jester, am I right?"

"He does," said Sally, covering Harry's hand with affection.

After brandies, a violinist and an accordion player appeared and spiritedly began to play folk music. The captain asked Harry's permission to dance with Sally. Harry said it was fine with him and watched his wife be taken off by the captain, who had placed a bearish arm around her shoulder. The combination of the heavy dinner and the motion of the ship made Harry ill. He asked if he might be excused. Sally looked at him with an appeal in her eyes and asked if he wanted her to come along. He said no, no, he'd be fine, and returned to the cabin where he fell asleep immediately in his clothes. When he awakened, he realized it was daybreak and Sally had not returned. He closed his eyes and, when she did appear, said nothing. Several hours later the ship docked briefly to take on fuel at a small and scruffy vacation island. Harry packed quietly and, after stopping for a moment to look at his sleeping wife and to touch her hair, left the ship. At a dockside shop that sold gold items at a discount, he found a phone and was easily able to get through to Rene Steinman.

He imagined him rolling over in his loft bed, turning his back on a neurotic actress.

"Who is it?" asked the director.

"It's Harry Towns. See if you can get a table tonight. I'm on my way."

THE CURRENT CLIMATE

* * *

After the play had opened and Harry had gotten a little attention, he told Wellman he felt it was time for him to push on.

"You are making a mistake," said the publisher, a comment that unsettled Harry. But then Wellman switched gears and decided to give a large farewell party for Harry at his home—which Harry, with the best of intentions, was unable to get to. He was upset about Sally and, on the day of the party, he kept driving aimlessly along Westchester highways. Finally, in the early evening, he called Wellman and said he was sorry but it didn't look as if he was going to make it.

"But thanks anyway," he said.

"Can you at least come over and look at my wife's antiques?" asked the publisher.

"I would," said Harry, "but there is no way I can find your house."

After resigning from the company, Harry moved out of the apartment he shared with Sally and began a long flirtation with Hollywood, one in which he would blushingly appear from time to time, allow his knee to be squeezed and then shyly return home, having never quite come across. What was he saving himself for? East Coast Seriousness? His Spanish Armada play? Or was it possible that in the style of great flirts, he felt he would be a disappointment if he actually jumped into bed and stayed the night? The work of actually getting movies made was hard and brutal, executed by low-slung men with plumber's hands who broke things and got down in the mud. It was no accident that it had all begun with Jewish immigrants from Eastern Europe. You had to want that cabinet and want to build it. Though he did not feel it qualified him for a benefit dinner, Harry preferred moonbeams. Didn't you hire other people to build cabinets? But who knows, maybe they liked moonbeams, too. Rough moonbeams.

In any case, Harry stayed out on the edges of the film business, turning up now and then to drink the orange juice and hustle the yellow-haired girls. He even backed into a few major credits which

183

put him on top for a few minutes. It was a nice feeling. And since there was only Harry to take care of, this glancing connection with the West Coast worked out fine. Matty had once offered him a quick rewrite. "It's a piece of cake," he had said. "All you have to do is get certain forces to converge."

"No thanks, Matty," Harry had said. "I have already earned my quota for this year."

Matty thought it was the weirdest thing anyone had ever said to him and dined out on it. But it made sense to Harry. Why accumulate dollars when you had enough of them to get by? And besides, he knew about those pieces of cake.

But then he spotted Julie one day getting out of a U.S. Post Office jeep with a sack of mail over her shoulder and he fell in love. And suddenly there was Megan and the animals and a lawn and the house that you had to hold on to at all costs.

So Harry sent the word out to Hollywood that he was finally ready to take off his clothes—and no one seemed to care. Who wanted to fuck an old broad. The offers stopped coming, and while Julie checked the real estate listings in Vermont, Harry signed on to do the television dog show which he could tell was not going to work out the second he saw the dog they had hired. It was a fat dog. But the trainer had green eyes and long hickory-colored hair so Harry didn't say anything and asked his friend Travis for a loan.

And then, just as he was wondering if the State Department ever hired washed-up screenwriters to man their lesser outposts, Harry suddenly found himself back on top.

Four

～～ HE STILL WASN'T A KEY PLAYER—IT wasn't as if he lunched with the brass at Orion—but he was on top enough for him. He was in position to clear out a whole drawerful of socks and not worry about matching them up someday. Just buy six basic new pairs. And swing his family down to the Fontainebleau Hotel in Miami Beach, after Julie, who sought out treats for him, suggested it might be fascinating. Thinking to economize, she had signed them up for a package deal; as a result, the Fontainebleau had put them in a toilet on the ground floor—with construction activity in their faces. Working with his new confidence, Harry was able to call the public-relations department and mention the names of a few pictures he had worked on, ones that everyone had seen.

"I don't usually do this," he had told the nice young woman he spoke to. And strictly speaking, someone else should have made the call on his behalf. Julie, for example. But the tactic got them upgraded to a real thumper on the tenth floor where the wind was so fierce, you risked being yanked off the terrace—and you could practically see the dope being flown in from Panama. Harry had been told there was menace in the air in Miami Beach—and he did pick up a trace of it here and there—in one cab, for example. But what he saw for the most part were Brazilian women with tushes exploding out of their bikinis and Frenchmen who craned their heads in innocence while at the same time sneaking ahead of you on restaurant lines. He did see an entire shark being rushed somewhere on a room-service trolley. So Miami Beach was probably fascinating, although not as much as he had been led to believe.

He bought Julie a gold pin for Valentine's Day instead of just another blouse that would get sucked up in her closet. He wasn't that surefooted when it came to jewelry, but the gold had been fashioned into lace and twisted up into a bow. Because he was back on top, he was able to get the salesman to hack off a substantial part of the price. Julie gave every evidence of loving it and wore it that night to a Cajun restaurant. He got Megan a couple of baronial castles, possibly influenced by all the Germans at the Fontainebleau.

Harry's friend Travis had agreed to lend him some money—which Harry suddenly didn't need. So he called Travis to tell him not to send it. When Travis heard Harry's voice, he missed the point and thought Harry was about to ask him to rush off a check. He spoiled things a little by saying in an anguished wail: "I'll give you fifty and then my sister will want fifty—and soon I'll have nothing." But Harry assured him he didn't need the money and told Travis he still couldn't get over how moved he was by his friend's offer. Travis countered by saying: "But you offered to come and stay with me in the hospital when I thought I was dying." Harry didn't remember making that offer and frankly couldn't imagine himself doing such a thing—staying away from Julie and Megan for an extended period of time—but he took his friend's word for it.

What had happened is that the network decided to pick up Harry's dog show, after all. Even though they had a similar show in development—one that featured a famous dog—they came to the conclusion that Harry's was more humanistic. So they ordered up twelve of them. Harry wasn't so sure he wanted to work on that many dog shows—but he had learned that in this business you took what you got. And, of all things, Matty had gotten wind of Harry's abortive Spanish Armada play and felt there was a movie in it. If you focused on the period when they were trying to get the Armada together. And stopped at the dock, just before it set sail. That way you wouldn't have to worry about the actual Armada. You wouldn't have to round up urcas. It wasn't what Harry had in mind, but at least he'd be able to salvage some of his Armada research.

It kept coming. He was offered a small role in a movie—as the brother of a cockfighter. The cockfighter himself was to be played by a fine English actor whose name wasn't instantly recognizable but whose face you would know in a second if you were a student of BBC productions. Julie knew who he was immediately. It caught Harry at a good time, so he said what the hell. At the shooting the English actor was a little frosty, but he gradually warmed up and even gave Harry an acting tip—showing him how to lean in toward a person with a little rotation of one hand to simulate an intimate conversation. Even if you weren't having one. Harry told a friend of his about the experience and the friend said, "It beats the hell out of writing." Harry went around saying the same thing, that acting beat the hell out of writing.

There was no end to his good fortune. An Italian film scholar wrote Harry and told him she had found a thread of continuity in his screenwork, one that got tangled up in the seventies. Still, she said that she would like to follow that thread. Harry got off a letter to Bologna telling her to be his guest.

So Harry was finally able to take a deep breath and not have to worry about selling his house and moving up to Vermont. Having to make Vermont friends. He had been having a property dispute with a neighbor who picked up Harry's property sign—it read H. TOWNS—and stuck it back in close to Harry's house, where he felt it should be. Harry had been too dispirited to do anything about it and just let it sit there. He told himself there wasn't anything important about where a sign got stuck in. But then the dog show got picked up and the letter came from Bologna, and the acting fell in. He found himself wandering over to the sign, yanking it out and sticking it back in where *he* felt it should be. Strictly speaking, he had stuck it closer to the neighbor's house than the deed allowed.

Now that the breaks were coming his way again, Harry couldn't help but wonder what had caused his slide—and what had arrested it.

Harry Towns had written a love story. It was based on his romance with Julie, which he often felt a need to announce was not perfect. Actually he felt it *was* perfect, but he didn't want to jinx it. So he said it wasn't. Every now and then Julie would slip and start to knock them back. Or Harry would dope down and be out of reach for a couple of nights. But he papered over these aspects of the romance and focused on the perfect part. He and the producer had not gotten along—possibly dating back to the night he had picked up the producer and his wife in his arms and danced them around a disco. He was feeling his oats that night. He may even have slipped a tongue in the producer's wife's mouth, but he didn't want to think about that. The producer had accepted his show of high spirits stoically, but there was no doubt in Harry's mind that he had filed it away. And next thing he knew, Harry was off the picture. He was notified of this by a waiter at Elaine's restaurant in New York City. In other words, he was the last to know. He felt this was tacky of the producer, who should have fired him to his face. Still, he had to concede that some people had trouble with that type of confrontation.

A husband-and-wife comedy team had been called in to punch up Harry's script. The picture, considered a sleeper, had gone on to become a success at the box office. And it had been put up for an award. The producer, no doubt having to screw up his courage to do so, had called Harry and asked him to fly out and be present for the award ceremony. Then he added: "You won't be getting many more of these." Harry should have shot back: "What about you, you little fuck?" But he tended to be a little late with his rejoinders. What he shot back with was that he would go if his expenses were paid.

So Harry and his family flew out there and checked into the Beverly Hills Hotel. He had to set aside his Spanish Armada play, which probably wasn't the worst thing in the world, since he still hadn't been able to get any tension into it.

THE CURRENT CLIMATE

Julie's friend, Cyma, bused up from San Diego to baby-sit for Megan. She was an unreconstructed hippie and brought along a little bags of nuts and berries. Her legs were hairy, but the hotel let her in, anyway. Harry had his usual debate over whether to "take down" the gray in his hair and decided, as he always did, to put it off for a while. If he showed up suddenly with Alan King hair, it would send the wrong signal to the industry. The tuxedo bunched up his neck fat, but overall he thought he looked fine. Julie had chunked up a bit in the shoulders, but as usual, her aristocratic bones pulled her through. She had told Harry about these bones when they first started dating.

The main thing is how formidable he felt when she was around. What if he lost her? Even thinking about it made him have to hold on to something.

He hired a limo to take them to the awards ceremony, even though, strictly speaking, it had not been negotiated as part of his deal. They got to the ceremony early. Only one couple was there before them. The man wore a tuxedo and the woman did, too, only hers was a larger-than-life version of one that somehow tied in with Liza Minnelli. They darted in and out of alcoves and seemed anxious for the ceremony to get under way. Julie guessed they were the husband-and-wife comedy team that had punched up Harry's script, and as it turned out, she was right. A few writers arrived with their wives. They seemed a scruffy and amiable lot, causing Julie and Harry to wonder if maybe they ought to move out to the Coast and get in on their softball games and seminars. The trouble with Harry and Julie is that they wanted to live in every place they visited.

The producer had taken a table for himself, the director, the husband-and-wife comedy team, and Harry and Julie if they showed up, which they did. Harry thought he would break the ice by reaching across to congratulate the husband-and-wife team on the job they had done of punching up his script. Not that he liked it that much. They had thrown in some scenes that he felt were sniggering. You could argue that the sniggering scenes helped the

191

picture with young audiences, but Harry didn't see it that way. He felt that if they had shot the picture as is, it would have reached young and old audiences alike. It would still be in the theaters. And he didn't automatically feel that way about his work. But he didn't say all that. He simply reached across to shake hands with them, even though he felt they had stunk up his script. They responded stiffly and turned to watch the ceremonies. The men in charge of the program bounced out one by one and did Carson-style one-liners. They appeared to be serious individuals, but they seemed to feel there was a need for them to do this.

It was at this point that Harry became aware that the husband-and-wife team were pouting at him. They had been joined at the table by their teenage son and daughter, who did backup pouts. What were they so upset about? There had been a dispute over whose name should be on the picture. They felt they had punched up Harry's script to the extent that it was their script, not Harry's. And that they deserved full credit for it. Harry had had to fly out to the Coast and remind everyone that it was *his* script they had punched up. You *did* have to have something to punch up, didn't you? So they had wound up all crowded together in the credits.

Harry felt their anger, too, which came as a surprise to him. Possibly it was because he had never run into a mass pout before. Later Julie was to say that she had never seen anything like it. So it wasn't his imagination. The director was correct in his behavior, but Harry recalled that he had given an interview to the trades, in which he said that Harry didn't know spit about how to write a second act. Which presumably set him apart from other American writers. He could understand the director feeling this way— but why announce it to the industry, thereby jeopardizing Harry's livelihood? So the director was sort of in on it too. The producer had parlayed the picture into seventeen deals. Everybody in the industry wanted to work with him. So even though he sat at the table, he was more or less off by himself, shining with success.

It got to the point that Harry didn't know if he wanted to win the award or not. He would have liked to thank Julie for her support. The thrust of the acceptance speech he had roughed out was that she had practically carried him on her back. But did he really want to waltz up there with the producer and the husband-and-wife comedy team—as if they were one big happy family?

So he was almost relieved when they lost. The winner was a client of Pauli Smetler, a Hungarian of almost legendary charm who had, until recently, represented Harry. When Harry left him—he felt he wasn't getting enough action and joined a bigger agency—Pauli said: "You have broken my heart," which made Harry feel awful. Julie adored Pauli and loved his Lotte Lenya anecdotes but felt it was unprofessional of him to guilt-trip Harry. When the winner was announced, a studio executive who had also become a legend—in this case for his hard-driving work habits—jumped up on Pauli and wrapped his legs around him—at some jeopardy, Harry felt, to the old man's health. With the studio executive still on him, Pauli somehow managed to inch his way toward Harry and say: "Let's not forget Mr. Towns, a fine talent." The studio executive got down off Pauli and said "Let's do something" to Harry, who felt the offer lacked enthusiasm. The executive then congratulated the husband-and-wife team on the house they had bought in Malibu.

"Good, good," he said. "Extend yourself. That way you'll have to work harder for me."

So Harry felt awful. Everybody had twenty deals going, they were wrapping their legs around his ex-agent, and he was sitting there, trying to look confident, with a Spanish Armada play that didn't have any inherent conflict in it. The wife in the husband-and-wife comedy team broke ranks and told Harry she had always admired a line in one of his films. She said it in the manner of a fresh young talent being deferential to someone who is being phased out. As it turned out, Harry hadn't written the line, even though his name was on the picture. Besides, it was too late for all that. There was a party at Spago, but Harry just wanted to get out of there and go back to the hotel. Julie felt the same way.

On the sidewalk, as they waited for the limo, Harry's niece

193

Daisy, who had M.S., materialized in the moonlight. She was in and out of schools in the area and was a show-biz freak—so it was no surprise that she had found out about the ceremony.

She came forward with a woman who had a wide face and carried a clipboard.

"This is my Uncle Harry," she said. "He knows people like Tom Cruise and Dustin Hoffman."

Daisy could embarrass the hell out of you, but you couldn't come down too hard on her because of the M.S. It was the kind that didn't show, but still . . .

"Do you know people like that?" the woman asked.

"Not really," said Harry, who did not give her a flat-out no.

The woman made a notation on her clipboard and slipped back into a thin little group that was waiting for stars.

Daisy had heard about the party at Spago and begged Harry to take her to it. He sensed it was a bad idea, but he allowed himself to be pushed into the limo—and all of a sudden they were on their way. There was a small element of showing off in his indecision.

The limo driver accompanied them to the door and gave Harry's name to the woman with the invitation list. Harry stood by uneasily, while the woman looked for his name.

"It's not on here," she said.

"That's ridiculous," said Daisy, who began to reel off Harry's credits, giving him sole authorship of pictures he had only cowritten. He was pissed off at her but had to hold off because of the MS.

Harry told the woman he had been to the restaurant a dozen times with Sid and Matty. The woman acknowledged that she knew them but insisted the party was by invitation only. Julie began to tug at his arm, but Harry yanked it away and said that for Christ's sakes, he had just come from an award ceremony and was a runner-up. The woman said that had nothing to do with it. She didn't even have the good grace to be rude. And then he did something he swore he'd never do—*he* began hollering out his credits. A couple of heavy hitters who really had some came by and made faces at the commotion—before they were waved in. Running out of gas, Harry lowered his voice and asked the woman to call up Matty or Sid, one of whom would surely vouch for him. She said she didn't see any point to it.

"It doesn't look as if we're going to get in," he told Julie.

"Big deal," she said.

"That's how I feel."

The limo driver said he knew of a party for a group of second-unit people in Culver City, but Harry said they weren't interested in that.

Through the restaurant window he caught a glimpse of Pauli, who was talking to the producer. It was a good thing he didn't see the husband-and-wife comedy team, although they may have been in there. Pauli spread his arms as if to say: "What's going on?" and then walked toward the door to help out. But Harry turned away and headed for the limo, no doubt breaking the old man's heart again. He seemed fated to keep breaking it, over and over again. Before they got into the car, they saw Daisy slip past the woman at the door and sit down with Telly Savalas.

By all rights, they should have gotten on a plane and gone home. But Harry figured as long as they were out there, why not try to get something going? He needed a win. When the picture opened, Harry, instead of scooping up a couple of assignments, had perversely embarked on his Spanish Armada play despite its inherent lack of conflict. He needed to do something serious. But apart from being blown off-course at Corunna, nothing happened to the Armada. He even tried to make that the point—that nothing happened, giving it an absurdist spin—but people weren't going to fork over fifty dollars to have that point made. And Harry wasn't about to tamper with history. He did that in the movies.

In the meanwhile the producer of Harry's love story had parlayed it into his seventeen deals. The husband-and-wife comedy team, having obviously been credited with the picture's success, were working their asses off. Also, a bunch of crisp, wafer-thin fellows with the reputation of not doing coke and working from

195

dawn to midnight had quietly slipped into key positions in the industry. Fellows that Harry didn't know. This is the atmosphere in which he had to play catch-up.

When Harry left Pauli, he had signed with an octopuslike agency and been turned over to a crisp, wafer-thin fellow of his own. The agent always asked how Julie and Megan were doing, but it was as if he were following the guidelines of a course in client relations. Harry called him up to see if there was anything around, and the agent told him there was a rewrite job at one of the studios. If Harry and the executive in charge got along, the agent, using the full force of his organization, might be able to ram Harry through. Harry said he didn't particularly care to be rammed through, but the agent didn't follow him on that and asked how Julie and Megan were getting along.

Harry went over to see the studio executive, who turned out to be a stocky gay guy with a brush mustache and parachute pants.

"If only we could get you," the fellow said, coming out to greet Harry in the reception area.

"You've got me," said Harry.

"I'll be right with you," said the executive. But he wasn't right with Harry. He kept him waiting for two hours. Why Harry stuck around, he would never know. He needed a job, but this went way past the point of humiliation. He'd heard that certain studios beat you up. Maybe that's what they were doing, beating him up. What was the point of it? he wondered. There was always the chance that the fellow wanted to clear out his calls so that he could give Harry his full attention. But from where he sat, Harry could get the gist of the calls, which were about restaurants. So Harry finally said fuck it and left. There was nothing courageous about this. It was self-preservation. He started to have trouble breathing. And he didn't want to be found dead in the outer office of some faggot in parachute pants. It was not the kind of send-off he had in mind.

He went back to the hotel and tried to concentrate on a board game with Megan. It's possible he had blown another studio, but so what? There would be another crowd in there in six months, anyway. The agent called and said he understood Harry's feelings but that he needed a picture. Harry said he didn't *need* anything. There were plenty of people walking around leading perfectly happy lives without a picture. He had other options. And he did, too, even if one of them was to sell his house, move up to Vermont, and become a woodcutter.

Julie told him not to worry, he had his Armada play. But she was just saying that. She had been hearing about the play from the day they'd met and knew perfectly well it lacked dramatic tension. And was that really going to bail them out—Harry's play about the Spanish Armada.

Matty came by that night. Harry knew how busy he was, so he appreciated the gesture, even though it had the look of a condolence call. Matty had been having trouble with his fourth wife, the one he thought was finally going to do it for him, and was subdued, but the visit showed that he really cared about Harry and his family.

"This means a lot to me," said Harry when the subdued visit was over.

"Hey, I really love you," said Matty, giving Harry a hug. And Harry would never forget his kindness.

They decided to spend their last night at Chasen's. Since it was an old-line Hollywood restaurant, Harry had a feeling it would be out of favor with the crisp new executives who had taken over key positions in the industry. Julie dressed in the gown she'd worn to the awards ceremony, using different accessories so that it would look like a new outfit. Harry's main course had capers all over it and was probably a little too rich for him. So he went into the john to see if he wanted to throw up. Maybe it was because he was generally upset. Muhammad Ali was at one of the urinals. Harry went crazy when he saw him. He had done a documentary on the young Joe Frazier and had gotten close to the fighter, with the result that he had to show solidarity with him through all the great fights with Ali. He took the position that Ali's skills were God-given, whereas Frazier, a former fat boy, had had to earn his. But

197

his heart had always been with Ali. Letting out a whole week's worth of frustration, he told Ali he was the greatest athlete he had ever seen in *any* sport and that he couldn't possibly understand what it meant for Harry to be standing there in the john with him at Chasen's. He saluted Ali's stance on Vietnam and told him he could never understand the controversy over his win against Liston in Lewiston. He even began to chant "Al-i, Al-i," as if he were in the stands watching the Thrilla at Manila.

"Who are you, man?" asked Ali at the urinal. Harry said he was a screenwriter and mentioned a few of his credits. But he told Ali that his credits were beside the point. The only thing that mattered was that this was the most exciting moment in his life. He only wished his father could have been there with him.

"Well, God bless you, man," said Ali.

The two men hugged each other and Harry began to cry.

He went back to the table and told Julie what had happened. She said she was happy for him, but knowing Harry, she was also concerned about whether the poor man had gotten to take a leak. Harry said he felt confident that he had. And he wouldn't let go of what had happened. Here he was, making a big deal out of being frozen out of the industry, and then all of a sudden he gets to throw his arms around Muhammad Ali at a urinal at Chasen's. He said it put everything in perspective, and he started to cry again.

Ali came out of the john and hugged a fellow Harry recognized as being a key player in the mini-series business. This threw Harry off temporarily—but he still had that moment and he felt better and he told Julie she had no idea what it meant to him and that no one would ever be able to take it away. He even forgot to vomit.

It would be nice to report that Harry's luck changed after the epiphany in the john at Chasen's. But it didn't work that way. He flew home with a sinking heart, anyway, feeling he had left behind a huge entertainment metropolis, one that throbbed with activity and yet had no place in it for him. After his thirty-five years in the business.

THE CURRENT CLIMATE

He didn't have to wait long, though. Matty, who was scouting locations in the area, dropped by with a blond streak and a boy in tow. After four broken marriages he had decided to try being a little gay. Which was all right with Harry. Nor was he surprised. Matty had once broken into a twitchy little walk around the room, which embarrassed Harry and probably signaled the start of his gay phase. The boy sat in the other room while Harry steered the conversation around to his Spanish Armada play. Julie claimed he would do that to strangers on the street.

Matty let it sink in and said: "You sonofabitch, you've got me hooked." He said it as if it were the last thing he wanted to have happen to him. They smoked a joint, and then Matty, who always boasted he could sell shit in a brown bag, got a studio executive out of bed on a Sunday morning and pitched him the story. And Harry suddenly had a deal. Even though Matty left out the critical role played by Philip II. Then the network ordered up his dog show, the letter came from Bologna, the acting job fell in—and Harry was back on top.

He had to be careful this time. Not piss it away. Trust old friends and take what was given to him. Don't be a wise guy. It could all unravel so quickly.

He was going back to the Armada, though. The real Armada, not just the events that led up to it. If Matty felt there was a picture in the *financing* of the Armada, fine, he wasn't going to argue with him. But Harry had a date with the voyage itself. That's what had attracted him in the first place. He'd go back to it the first time he got six months ahead, a solid six months this time, so that he didn't have to look over his shoulder for the accountant. The dog show would give him financial security. Why let Julie and Megan hang out to dry?

There was still the question of conflict. But how could it not exist in an enterprise that size? He just hadn't found it yet. But he would.

There was such a thing as cutting bait, taking your losses. He had done that on the Siege of Malta, when he had found himself

199

sympathizing with the Turks. But not on this baby. He didn't want to wake up and be seventy-five and look in the mirror and see a man with white hair and rotten teeth who'd backed away from a challenge. If necessary, he'd build up Drake or the quirky Duke of Parma. Maybe throw in a girl. You could argue that this wasn't historically accurate. But who the hell knew what went on in the sixteenth century? The main thing is—he'd crack that sonofabitch if he had to take twenty runs at it and kill himself in the process. Otherwise, fuck it, let somebody else be on top.